D1417105

Mac Donald, George   F- MacD
AUTHOR   L
Lady of the Mansion
TITLE
#4497

Mac Donald   F- MacD
#4497   L
    Lady of the mansion

LADY OF THE MANSION

Lady
of the
Mansion

Originally published as THE PORTENT

George MacDonald

1817

HARPER & ROW, PUBLISHERS, San Francisco
Cambridge, Hagerstown, New York, Philadelphia
London, Mexico City, São Paulo, Sydney

Originally published as THE PORTENT.

Library of Congress Cataloging in Publication Data

MacDonald, George, 1824–1905.
    LADY OF THE MANSION.

    I. Title.
PR4967.P67   1983   823'.8   82-48944
ISBN 0-06-250564-5 (pbk.)

87   10 9 8 7 6

Contents

LADY OF THE MANSION

CHAPTER 1

My Boyhood

M<small>Y</small> father belonged to the widespread family of the Campbells, and possessed a small landed property in the north of Argyll. But although of long descent and high connection, he was no richer than many a farmer of a few hundred acres. For, with the exception of a narrow belt of arable land at its foot, a bare hill formed almost the whole of his possessions. The sheep ate over it, and no doubt found it good; I bounded and climbed all over it, and thought it a kingdom. From my very childhood, I had rejoiced in being alone. The sense of room about me had been one of my greatest delights. Hence, when my thoughts go back to those old years, it is not the house, nor the family room, nor that in which I slept, that first of all rises before my inward vision, but that desolate hill, the top of which was only a wide expanse of moorland, rugged with height and hollow, and dangerous with deep, dark pools, but in many portions purple with large-belled heather, and crowded with cranberry and blaeberry plants. Most of all, I loved it in the still autumn morning, outstretched in stillness, high uplifted towards the heaven. On every stalk hung the dew in tiny drops, which, while the rising sun was low, sparkled and burned with the hues of all the gems. Here and there a bird gave a cry; no other sound awoke the silence. I never see the statue of the Roman youth, praying with outstretched arms, and open, empty, level palms, as waiting to receive and hold the blessing of the gods, but that outstretched barren heath rises before me, as if it meant the same thing as the statue—or were, at least, the fit room in the middle space of which to set the praying and expectant youth.

There was one spot upon the hill, half-way between the valley and the moorland, which was my favourite haunt. This part of the hill was covered with great blocks of stone, of all shapes and sizes—here crowded together, like the slain where the battle had been fiercest; there parting asunder from spaces of delicate green—of softest grass. In the centre of one of these green spots, on a steep part of the hill, were three huge rocks—two projecting out of the hill, rather than standing up from it, and one, likewise projecting from the hill, but lying across the tops of the two, so as to form a little cave, the back of which was the side of the hill. This was my refuge, my home within a home, my study—and, in the hot noons, often my sleeping chamber, and my house of dreams. If the wind blew cold on the hillside, a hollow of lulling warmth was there, scooped as it were out of the body of the blast, which, sweeping around, whistled keen and thin through the cracks and crannies of the rocky chaos that lay all about; in which confusion of rocks the wind plunged, and flowed, and eddied, and withdrew, as the sea-waves on the cliffy shores or the unknown rugged bottoms. Here I would often lie, as the sun went down, and watch the silent growth of another sea, which the stormy ocean of the wind could not disturb—the sea of the darkness. First it would begin to gather in the bottom of hollow places. Deep valleys, and all little pits on the hillsides, were wellsprings where it gathered, and whence it seemed to overflow, till it had buried the earth beneath its mass, and, rising high into the heavens, swept over the faces of the stars, washed the blinding day from them, and let them shine, down through the waters of the dark, to the eyes of men below. I would lie till nothing but the stars and the dim outlines of hills against the sky was to be seen, and then rise and go home, as sure of my path as if I had been descending a dark staircase in my father's house.

On the opposite side the valley, another hill lay parallel to mine; and behind it, at some miles' distance, a great mountain. As often as, in my hermit's cave, I lifted my eyes from the volume I was reading, I saw this mountain before me. Very different was its character from that of the hill on which I was seated. It was a mighty thing, a chieftain of the race, seamed and scarred, featured with chasms and precipices and overleaning rocks, themselves huge as hills; here blackened with shade, there overspread with glory; interlaced with the silvery lines of falling streams, which, hurrying from heaven to earth, cared not how they went, so it were downwards. Fearful stories were told of the gulfs, sullen waters, and dizzy heights upon that terror-haunted mountain. In storms the wind roared like thunder in its caverns and along the jagged sides of its cliffs, but at other times that uplifted land—uplifted, yet secret and full of dismay—lay silent as a cloud on the horizon.

I had a certain peculiarity of constitution, which I have some reason to believe I inherit. It seems to have its root in an unusual delicacy of hearing, which often conveys to me sounds inaudible to those about me. This I have had many opportunities of proving. It has likewise, however, brought me sounds which I could never trace back to their origin; though they may have arisen from some natural operation which I had not perseverance or mental acuteness sufficient to discover. From this, or, it may be, from some deeper cause with which this is connected, arose a certain kind of fearfulness associated with the sense of hearing, of which I have never heard a corresponding instance. Full as my mind was of the wild and sometimes fearful tales of a Highland nursery, fear never entered my mind by the eyes; nor, when I brooded over tales of terror, and fancied new and yet more frightful embodiments of horror, did I shudder at any imaginable spectacle, or tremble lest the fancy should become fact, and from behind the whin-bush or the elder-hedge should glide forth the tall swaying form of the Boneless. When alone in bed, I used to lie awake, and look out into the room, peopling it with the forms of all the persons who had died within the scope of my memory and acquaintance. These fancied forms were vividly present to my imagination. I pictured them pale, with dark circles around their hollow eyes, visible by a light which glimmered within them; not the light of life, but a pale, greenish phosphorescence, generated by the decay of the brain inside. Their garments were white and trailing, but torn and soiled, as by trying often in vain to get up out of the buried coffin. But so far from being terrified by these imaginings, I used to delight in them; and in the long winter evenings, when I did not happen to have any book that interested me sufficiently, I used even to look forward with expectation to the hour when, laying myself straight upon my back, as if my bed were my coffin, I could call up from underground all who had passed away, and see how they fared, yea, what progress they had made towards final dissolution of form—but all the time, with my fingers pushed hard into my ears, lest the faintest sound should invade the silent citadel of my soul. If inadvertently I removed one of my fingers, the agony of terror I instantly experienced is indescribable. I can compare it to nothing but the rushing in upon my brain of a whole churchyard of spectres. The very possibility of hearing a sound, in such a mood, and at such a time, was almost enough to paralyse me. So I could scare myself in broad daylight, on the open hillside, by imagining unintelligible sounds; and my imagination was both original and fertile in the invention of such. But my mind was too active to be often subjected to such influences. Indeed life would have been hardly endurable had these moods been of more than occasional occurrence. As I grew older, I almost outgrew them. Yet sometimes one awful dread would seize me—that, perhaps, the prophetic power manifest in the gift of second sight, which, according to the testimony of my old nurse, had belonged to several of my ancestors, had been in my case transformed in kind without losing its nature, transferring its abode from the sight to the hearing, whence resulted its keenness, and my fear and suffering.

CHAPTER 2

The Second Hearing

ONE summer evening, I had lingered longer than usual in my rocky retreat: I had lain half dreaming in the mouth of my cave, till the shadows of evening had fallen, and the gloaming had deepened half-way towards the night. But the night had no more terrors for me than the day. Indeed, in such regions there is a solitariness for which there seems a peculiar sense, and upon which the shadows of night sink with a strange relief, hiding from the eye the wide space which yet they throw more open to the imagination. When I lifted my head, only a star here and there caught my eye; but, looking intently into the depths of blue-grey, I saw that they were crowded with twinkles. The mountain rose before me, a huge mass of gloom; but its several peaks stood out against the sky with a clear, pure, sharp outline, and looked nearer to me than the bulk from which they rose heavenwards. One star trembled and throbbed upon the very tip of the loftiest, the central peak, which seemed the spire of a mighty temple where the light was worshipped—crowned, therefore, in the darkness, with the emblem of the day. I was lying, as I have said, with this fancy still in my thought, when suddenly I heard, clear, though faint and far away, the sound as of the iron-shod hoofs of a horse, in furious gallop along an uneven rocky surface. It was more like a distant echo than an original sound. It seemed to come from the face of the mountain, where no horse, I knew, could go at that speed, even if its rider courted certain destruction. There was a peculiarity, too, in the sound—a certain tinkle, or clank, which I fancied myself able, by auricular analysis, to distinguish from the body of the sound. Supposing the sound to be caused by the feet of a horse, the peculiarity was just such as would result from one of the shoes being loose. A terror—strange even to my experience—seized me, and I hastened home. The sounds gradually died away as I descended the hill. Could they have been an echo from some precipice of the mountain? I knew of no road lying so that, if a horse were galloping upon it, the sounds would be reflected from the mountain to me.

The next day, in one of my rambles, I found myself near the cottage of my old foster-mother, who was distantly related to us, and was a trusted servant in the family at the time I was born. On the death of my mother, which took place almost immediately after my birth, she had taken the entire charge of me, and had brought me up, though with difficulty; for she used to tell me, I

should never be either *folk* or *fairy*. For some years she
had lived alone in a cottage, at the bottom of a deep
green circular hollow, upon which, in walking over a
healthy table-land, one came with a sudden surprise. I
was her frequent visitor. She was a tall, thin, aged
woman, with eager eyes, and well-defined clear-cut features. Her voice was harsh, but with an undertone of
great tenderness. She was scrupulously careful in her
attire, which was rather above her station. Altogether,
she had much the bearing of a gentlewoman. Her devotion to me was quite motherly. Never having had any
family of her own, although she had been the wife of one
of my father's shepherds, she expended the whole mater-
nity of her nature upon me. She was always my first
resource in any perplexity, for I was sure of all the help
she could give me. And as she had much influence with
my father, who was rather severe in his notions, I had had
occasion to beg her interference. No necessity of this
sort, however, had led to my visit on the present occasion.

I ran down the side of the basin, and entered the little
cottage. Nurse was seated on a chair by the wall, with her
usual knitting, a stocking, in one hand; but her hands
were motionless, and her eyes wide open and fixed. I
knew that the neighbours stood rather in awe of her, on
the ground that she had the second sight; but, although
she often told us frightful enough stories, she had never
alluded to such a gift as being in her possession. Now I
concluded at once that she was *seeing*. I was confirmed in
this conclusion when, seeming to come to herself suddenly, she covered her head with her plaid, and sobbed

audibly, in spite of her efforts to command herself. But I did not dare to ask her any questions, nor did she attempt any excuse for her behaviour. After a few moments, she unveiled herself, rose, and welcomed me with her usual kindness; then got me some refreshment, and began to question me about matters at home. After a pause, she said suddenly: "When are you going to get your commission, Duncan, do you know?" I replied that I had heard nothing of it; that I did not think my father had influence or money enough to procure me one, and that I feared I should have no such good chance of distinguishing myself. She did not answer, but nodded her head three times, slowly and with compressed lips—apparently as much as to say, "I know better."

Just as I was leaving her, it occurred to me to mention that I had heard an odd sound the night before. She turned towards me, and looked at me fixedly. "What was it like, Duncan, my dear?"

"Like a horse galloping with a loose shoe," I replied.

"Duncan, Duncan, my darling!" she said, in a low, trembling voice, but with passionate earnestness, "you did not hear it? Tell me that you did not hear it! You only want to frighten poor old nurse: some one has been telling you the story!"

It was my turn to be frightened now; for the matter became at once associated with my fears as to the possible nature of my auricular peculiarities. I assured her that nothing was farther from my intention than to frighten her; that, on the contrary, she had rather alarmed me; and I begged her to explain. But she sat down white and trembling, and did not speak. Presently, however, she rose again, and saying, "I have known it happen sometimes without anything very bad following," began to put away the basin and plate I had been using, as if she would compel herself to be calm before me. I renewed my entreaties for an explanation, but without avail. She begged me to be content for a few days, as she was quite unable to tell the story at present. She promised, however, of her own accord, that before I left home she would tell me all she knew.

The next day a letter arrived announcing the death of a distant relation, through whose influence my father had had a lingering hope of obtaining an appointment for me. There was nothing left but to look out for a situation as tutor.

CHAPTER 3

My Old Nurse's Story

I was now almost nineteen. I had completed the usual curriculum of study at one of the Scotch universities; and, possessed of a fair knowledge of mathematics and physics, and what I considered rather more than a good foundation for classical and metaphysical acquirement, I resolved to apply for the first suitable situation that offered. But I was spared the trouble. A certain Lord Hilton, an English nobleman, residing in one of the midland counties, having heard that one of my father's sons was desirous of such a situation, wrote to him, offering me the post of tutor to his two boys, of the ages of ten and twelve. He had been partly educated at a Scotch university; and this, it may be, had prejudiced him in favour of a Scotch tutor; while an ancient alliance of the families by marriage was supposed by my nurse to be the reason of his offering me the situation. Of this connection, however, my father said nothing to me, and it went for nothing in my anticipations. I was to receive a hundred pounds a year, and to hold in the family the position of a gentleman, which might mean anything or nothing, according to the disposition of the heads of the family. Preparations for my departure were immediately commenced.

I set out one evening for the cottage of my old nurse, to bid her good-bye for many months, probably years. I was to leave the next day for Edinburgh, on my way to London, whence I had to repair by coach to my new abode—almost to me like the land beyond the grave, so little did I know about it, and so wide was the separation between it and my home. The evening was sultry when I began my walk, and before I arrived at its end, the clouds rising from all quarters of the horizon, and especially gathering around the peaks of the mountain, betokened the near approach of a thunderstorm. This was a great delight to me. Gladly would I take leave of my home with the memory of a last night of tumultuous magnificence; followed, probably, by a day of weeping rain, well suited to the mood of my own heart in bidding farewell to the best of parents and the dearest of homes. Besides, in common with most Scotchmen who are young and hardy enough to be unable to realise the existence of coughs and rheumatic fevers, it was a positive pleasure to me to be out in rain, hail, or snow.

"I am come to bid you good-bye, Margaret; and to hear the story which you promised to tell me before I left home: I go to-morrow."

"Do you go so soon, my darling? Well, it will be an awful night to tell it in; but, as I promised, I suppose I must."

At the moment, two or three great drops of rain, the first of the storm, fell down the wide chimney, exploding in the clear turf-fire.

"Yes, indeed you must," I replied.

After a short pause, she commenced. Of course she spoke in Gaelic; and I translate from my recollection of the Gaelic; but rather from the impression left upon my mind, than from any recollection of the words. She drew her chair near the fire, which we had reason to fear would soon be put out by the falling rain, and began.

"How old the story is, I do not know. It has come down through many generations. My grandmother told it to me as I tell it to you; and her mother and my mother sat beside, never interrupting, but nodding their heads at every turn. And it ought to begin like the fairy tales, *Once upon a time*—it took place so long ago; but it is too dreadful and too true to tell like a fairy tale. There were two brothers, sons of the chief of our clan, but as different in appearance and disposition as two men could be. The elder was fair-haired and strong, much given to hunting and fishing; fighting too, upon occasion, I dare say, when they made a foray upon the Saxon, to get back a mouthful of their own. But he was gentleness itself to every one about him, and the very soul of honour in all his doings. The younger was very dark in complexion, and tall and slender compared to his brother. He was very fond of book-learning, which, they say, was an uncommon taste in those times. He did not care for any sports or bodily exercises but one; and that, too, was unusual in these parts. It was horsemanship. He was a fierce rider, and as much at home in the saddle as in his study-chair. You may think that, so long ago, there was not much fit room for riding hereabouts; but, fit or not fit, he rode. From his reading and riding, the neighbours looked doubtfully upon him, and whispered about the black art. He usually bestrode a great powerful black horse, without a white hair on him; and people said it was either the devil himself, or a demon-horse from the devil's own stud. What favoured this notion was, that, in or out of the stable, the brute would let no other than his master go near him. Indeed, no one would venture, after he had killed two men, and grievously maimed a third, tearing him with his teeth and hoofs like a wild beast. But to his master he was obedient as a hound, and would even tremble in his presence sometimes.

"The youth's temper corresponded to his habits. He was both gloomy and passionate. Prone to anger, he had never been known to forgive. Debarred from anything on which he had set his heart, he would have gone mad with longing if he had not gone mad with rage. His soul was like the night around us now, dark, and sultry, and silent, but lighted up by the red levin of wrath, and torn by the bellowings of thunder-passion. He must have his will: hell might have his soul. Imagine, then, the rage and malice in his heart, when he suddenly became aware that an orphan girl, distantly related to them, who had lived with them for nearly two years, and whom he had loved for almost all that period, was loved by his elder brother, and loved him in return. He flung his right hand above his head, swore a terrible oath that if he might not, his brother should not, rushed out of the house, and galloped off among the hills.

"The orphan was a beautiful girl, tall, pale, and slender, with plentiful dark hair, which, when released from the snood, rippled down below her knees. Her appearance formed a strong contrast with that of her favoured lover, while there was some resemblance between her and the younger brother. This fact seemed, to his fierce selfishness, ground for a prior claim.

"It may appear strange that a man like him should not have had instant recourse to his superior and hidden knowledge, by means of which he might have got rid of his rival with far more of certainty and less of risk; but I presume that, for the moment, his passion overwhelmed his consciousness of skill. Yet I do not suppose that he foresaw the mode in which his hatred was about to operate. At the moment when he learned their mutual attachment, probably through a domestic, the lady was on her way to meet her lover as he returned from the day's sport. The appointed place was on the edge of a deep, rocky ravine, down in whose dark bosom brawled and foamed a little mountain torrent. You know the place, Duncan, my dear, I dare say."

(Here she gave me a minute description of the spot, with directions how to find it.)

"Whether any one saw what I am about to relate, or whether it was put together afterwards, I cannot tell. The story is like an old tree—so old that it has lost the marks of its growth. But this is how my grandmother told it to me. An evil chance led him in the right direction. The lovers, startled by the sound of the approaching horse, parted in opposite directions along a narrow mountain-path on the edge of the ravine. Into this path he struck at a point near where the lovers had met, but to opposite sides of which they had now receded; so that he was between them on the path. Turning his horse up the course of the stream, he soon came in sight of his brother on the ledge before him. With a suppressed scream of rage, he rode headlong at him, and ere he had time to make the least defence, hurled him over the precipice. The helplessness of the strong man was uttered in one single despairing cry as he shot into the abyss. Then all was still. The sound of his fall could not reach the edge of the gulf. Divining in a moment that the lady, whose name was Elsie, must have fled in the opposite direction, he reined his steed on his haunches. He could touch the precipice with his bridle-hand half outstretched; his sword-hand half outstretched would have dropped a stone to the bottom of the ravine. There was no room to wheel. One desperate practicability alone remained. Turning his horse's head towards the edge, he compelled him, by means of the powerful bit, to rear till he stood almost erect; and so, his body swaying over the gulf, with quivering and straining muscles, to turn on his hind-legs. Having completed the half-circle, he let him drop, and urged him furiously in the opposite direction. It must have been by the devil's own care that he was able to continue his gallop along that ledge of rock.

"He soon caught sight of the maiden. She was leaning, half fainting, against the precipice. She had heard her lover's last cry, and although it had conveyed no suggestion of his voice to her ear, she trembled from head to foot, and her limbs would bear her no farther. He checked his speed, rode gently up to her, lifted her unresisting, laid her across the shoulders of his horse, and, riding carefully till he reached a more open path, dashed again wildly along the mountain-side. The lady's long hair was shaken loose, and dropped trailing on the ground. The horse trampled upon it, and stumbled, half dragging her from the saddle-bow. He caught her, lifted her up, and looked at her face. She was dead. I suppose he went mad. He laid her again across the saddle before him, and rode on, reckless whither. Horse, and man, and maiden were found the next day, lying at the foot of a cliff, dashed to pieces. It was observed that a hind-shoe of the horse was loose and broken. Whether this had been the cause of his fall, could not be told; but ever when he races, as race he will, till the day of doom, along that mountain-side, his gallop is mingled with the clank of the loose and broken shoe. For, like the sin, the punishment is awful: he shall carry about for ages the phantom-body of the girl, knowing that her soul is away, sitting with the soul of his brother, down in the deep ravine, or scaling with him the topmost crags of the towering mountain-peaks. There are some who, from time to time, see the doomed man careering along the face of the mountain, with the lady hanging across the steed; and they say it always betokens a storm, such as this which is now raving around us."

I had not noticed till now, so absorbed had I been in her tale, that the storm had risen to a very ecstasy of fury.

"They say, likewise, that the lady's hair is still growing;

for, every time they see her, it is longer than before; and that now such is its length and the headlong speed of the horse, that it floats and streams out behind, like one of those curved clouds, like a comet's tail, far up in the sky; only the cloud is white, and the hair dark as night. And they say it will go on growing till the Last Day, when the horse will falter and her hair will gather in; and the horse will fall, and the hair will twist, and twine, and wreathe itself like a mist of threads about him, and blind him to everything but her. Then the body will rise up within it, face to face with him, animated by a fiend, who, twining *her* arms around him, will drag him down to the bottom-less pit."

I may mention something which now occurred, and which had a strange effect on my old nurse. It illustrates the assertion that we see around us only what is within us: marvellous things enough will show themselves to the marvellous mood. During a short lull in the storm, just as she had finished her story, we heard the sound of iron-shod hoofs approaching the cottage. There was no bridle-way into the glen. A knock came to the door, and, on opening it, we saw an old man seated on a horse, with a long slenderly-filled sack lying across the saddle before him. He said he had lost the path in the storm, and, seeing the light, had scrambled down to inquire his way. I perceived at once, from the scared and mysterious look of the old woman's eyes, that she was persuaded that this appearance had more than a little to do with the awful rider, the terrific storm, and myself who had heard the sound of the phantom-hoofs. As he ascended the hill, she looked after him, with wide and pale but unshrinking eyes; then turning in, shut and locked the door behind her, as by a natural instinct. After two or three of her significant nods, accompanied by the compression of her lips, she said:

"He need not think to take me in, wizard as he is, with his disguises. I can see him through them all. Duncan, my dear, when you suspect anything, do not be too incredulous. This human demon is of course a wizard still, and knows how to make himself, as well as anything he touches, take a quite different appearance from the real one; only every appearance must bear some resemblance, however distant, to the natural form. That man you saw at the door was the phantom of which I have been telling you. What he is after now, of course, I cannot tell; but you must keep a bold heart, and a firm and wary foot, as you go home to-night."

I showed some surprise, I do not doubt; and, perhaps, some fear as well; but I only said, "How do you know him, Margaret?"

"I can hardly tell you," she replied; "but I do know him. I think he hates me. Often, of a wild night, when there is moonlight enough by fits, I see him tearing around this little valley, just on the top edge—all round; the lady's hair and the horse's mane and tail driving far behind, and mingling, vaporous, with the stormy clouds. About he goes, in wild careering gallop; now lost as the moon goes in, then visible far round when she looks out again—an airy, pale-grey spectre, which few eyes but mine could see; for, as far as I am aware, no one of the family but myself has ever possessed the double gift of seeing and hearing both. In this case I hear no sound, except now and then a clank from the broken shoe. But I did not mean to tell you that I had ever seen him. I am not a bit afraid of him. He cannot do more than he may. His power is limited; else ill enough would he work, the miscreant."

"But," said I, "what has all this, terrible as it is, to do with the fright you took at my telling you that I had heard the sound of the broken shoe? Surely you are not afraid of only a storm?"

"No, my boy; I fear no storm. But the fact is, that that sound is seldom heard, and never, as far as I know, by any of the blood of that wicked man, without betokening some ill to one of the family, and most probably to the one who hears it—but I am not quite sure about that. Only some evil it does portend, although a long time may elapse before it shows itself; and I have a hope it may mean some one else than you."

"Do not wish that," I replied. "I know no one better able to bear it than I am; and I hope, whatever it may be, that I only shall have to meet it. It must surely be something serious to be so foretold—it can hardly be connected with my disappointment in being compelled to be a pedagogue instead of a soldier."

"Do not trouble yourself about that, Duncan," replied she. "A soldier you must be. The same day you told me of the clank of the broken horseshoe, I saw you return wounded from battle, and fall fainting from your horse in the street of a great city—only fainting, thank God. But I have particular reasons for being uneasy at *your* hearing that boding sound. Can you tell me the day and hour of your birth?"

"No," I replied. "It seems very odd when I think of it, but I really do not know even the day."

"Nor any one else; which is stranger still," she answered.

"How does that happen, nurse?"

"We were in terrible anxiety about your mother at the time. So ill was she, after you were just born, in a strange, unaccountable way, that you lay almost neglected for more than an hour. In the very act of giving birth to you, she seemed to the rest around her to be out of her mind, so wildly did she talk; but I knew better. I knew that she was fighting some evil power; and what power it was, I knew full well; for twice, during her pains, I heard the click of the horseshoe. But no one could help her. After her delivery, she lay as if in a trance, neither dead, nor at rest, but as if frozen to ice, and conscious of it all the while. Once more I heard the terrible sound of iron; and, at the moment, your mother started from her trance, screaming, 'My child! my child!' We suddenly became aware that no one had attended to the child, and rushed to the place where he lay wrapped in a blanket. Uncovering him, we found him black in the face, and spotted with dark spots upon the throat. I thought he was dead; but, with great and almost hopeless pains, we succeeded in making him breathe, and he gradually recovered. But his mother continued dreadfully exhausted. It seemed as if she had spent her life for her child's defence and birth. That was you, Duncan, my dear.

"I was in constant attendance upon her. About a week after your birth, as near as I can guess, just in the gloaming, I heard yet again the awful clank—only once. Nothing followed till about midnight. Your mother slept, and you lay asleep beside her. I sat by the bedside. A horror fell upon me suddenly, though I neither saw nor heard anything. Your mother started from her sleep with a cry, which sounded as if it came from far away, out of a dream, and did not belong to this world. My blood curdled with fear. She sat up in bed, with wide staring eyes and half-open rigid lips, and, feeble as she was, thrust her arms straight out before her with great force, her hands open and lifted up, with the palms outwards. The whole action was of one violently repelling another. She began to talk wildly as she had done before you were born, but, though I seemed to hear and understand it all at the time, I could not recall a word of it afterwards. It was as if I had listened to it when half asleep. I attempted to soothe her, putting my arms round her, but she seemed quite unconscious of my presence, and my arms seemed powerless upon the fixed muscles of hers. Not that I tried to constrain her, for I knew that a battle was going on of some kind or other, and my interference might do awful mischief. I only tried to comfort and encourage her. All the time, I was in a state of indescribable cold and suffering, whether more bodily or mental I could not tell. But at length I heard yet again the clank of the shoe. A sudden peace seemed to fall upon my mind—or was it a warm, odorous wind that filled the room? Your mother dropped her arms, and turned feebly towards her baby. She saw that he slept a blessed sleep. She smiled like a glorified spirit, and fell back exhausted on the pillow. I went to the other side of the room to get a cordial. When I returned to the bedside,

I saw at once that she was dead. Her face smiled still, with an expression of the uttermost bliss."

Nurse ceased, trembling as overcome by the recollection; and I was too much moved and awed to speak. At length, resuming the conversation, she said: "You see it is no wonder, Duncan, my dear, if, after all this, I should find, when I wanted to fix the date of your birth, that I could not determine the day or the hour when it took place. All was confusion in my poor brain. But it was strange that no one else could, any more than I. One thing only I can tell you about it. As I carried you across the room to lay you down, for I assisted at your birth, I happened to look up to the window. Then I saw what I did not forget, although I did not think of it again till many days after—a bright star was shining on the very tip of the thin crescent moon."

"Oh, then," said I, "it is possible to determine the day and the very hour when my birth took place."

"See the good of book-learning!" replied she. "When you work it out, just let me know, my dear, that I may remember it."

"That I will."

A silence of some moments followed. Margaret resumed:

"I am afraid you will laugh at my foolish fancies, Duncan; but in thinking over all these things, as you may suppose I often do, lying awake in my lonely bed, the notion sometimes comes to me: What if my Duncan be the youth whom his wicked brother hurled into the ravine, come again in a new body, to live out his life on the earth, cut short by his brother's hatred? If so, his persecution of you, and of your mother for your sake, is easy to understand. And if so, you will never be able to rest till you find your fere, wherever she may have been born on the face of the earth. For born she must be, long ere now, for you to find. I misdoubt me much, however, if you will find her without great conflict and suffering between, for the Powers of Darkness will be against you; though I have good hope that you will overcome at last. You must forgive the fancies of a foolish old woman, my dear."

I will not try to describe the strange feelings, almost sensations, that arose in me while listening to these extraordinary utterances, lest it should be supposed I was ready to believe all that Margaret narrated or concluded. I could not help doubting her sanity; but no more could I help feeling very peculiarly moved by her narrative.

Few more words were spoken on either side, but after receiving renewed exhortations to carefulness on my way home, I said good-bye to dear old nurse, considerably comforted, I must confess, that I was not doomed to be a tutor all my days; for I never questioned the truth of that vision and its consequent prophecy.

I went out into the midst of the storm, into the alternating throbs of blackness and radiance; now the possessor of no more room than what my body filled, and now isolated in world-wide space. And the thunder seemed to follow me, bellowing after me as I went.

Absorbed in the story I had heard, I took my way, as I thought, homewards. The whole country was well known to me. I should have said, before that night, that I could have gone home blindfold. Whether the lightning bewildered me and made me take a false turn, I cannot tell; for the hardest thing to understand, in intellectual as well as moral mistakes, is—how we came to go wrong. But after wandering for some time, plunged in meditation, and with no warning whatever of the presence of inimical powers, a brilliant lightning-flash showed me that at least I was not near home. The light was prolonged for a second or two by a slight electric pulsation; and by that I distinguished a wide space of blackness on the ground in front of me. Once more wrapped in the folds of a thick darkness, I dared not move. Suddenly it occurred to me what the blackness was, and whither I had wandered. It was a huge quarry, of great depth, long disused, and half filled with water. I knew the place perfectly. A few more steps would have carried me over the brink. I stood still, waiting for the next flash, that I might be quite sure of the way I was about to take before I ventured to move. While I stood, I fancied I heard a single hollow plunge in the black water far below. When the lightning came, I turned, and took my path in another direction.

After walking for some time across the heath, I fell. The fall became a roll, and down a steep declivity I went, over and over, arriving at the bottom uninjured.

Another flash soon showed me where I was—in the hollow valley, within a couple of hundred yards from nurse's cottage. I made my way towards it. There was no light in it, except the feeblest glow from the embers of her peat fire. "She is in bed," I said to myself, "and I will not disturb her." Yet something drew me towards the little window. I looked in. At first I could see nothing. At length, as I kept gazing, I saw something, indistinct in the darkness, like an outstretched human form.

By this time the storm had lulled. The moon had been up for some time, but had been quite concealed by tempestuous clouds. Now, however, these had begun to break up; and, while I stood looking into the cottage, they scattered away from the face of the moon, and a faint vapoury gleam of her light, entering the cottage through a window opposite that at which I stood, fell directly on the face of my old nurse, as she lay on her back, outstretched upon chairs, pale as death, and with her eyes closed. The light fell nowhere but on her face. A stranger to her habits would have thought she was dead; but she had so much of the appearance she had had on a former occasion, that I concluded at once she was in one of her trances. But having often heard that persons in such a condition ought not to be disturbed, and feeling quite sure she knew best how to manage herself, I turned, though reluctantly, and left the lone cottage behind me in the night, with the deathlike woman lying motionless in the midst of it.

I found my way home without any further difficulty, and went to bed, where I soon fell asleep, thoroughly wearied, more by the mental excitement I had been experiencing than by the amount of bodily exercise I had gone through.

My sleep was tormented with awful dreams; yet, strange to say, I awoke in the morning refreshed and fearless. The sun was shining through the chinks in my shutters, which had been closed because of the storm, and was making streaks and bands of golden brilliancy upon the wall. I had dressed and completed my preparations long before I heard the steps of the servant who came to call me.

What a wonderful thing waking is! The time of the ghostly moonshine passes by, and the great positive sunlight comes. A man who dreams, and knows that he is dreaming, thinks he knows what waking is; but knows it so little, that he mistakes, one after another, many a vague and dim change in his dream for an awaking. When the true waking comes at last, he is filled and overflowed with the power of its reality. So, likewise, one who, in the darkness, lies waiting for the light about to be struck, and trying to conceive, with all the force of his imagination, what the light will be like, is yet, when the reality flames up before him, seized as by a new and unexpected thing, different from and beyond all his imagining. He feels as if the darkness were cast to an infinite distance behind him. So shall it be with us when we wake from this dream of life into the truer life beyond, and find all our present notions of being, thrown back as into a dim, vapoury region of dreamland, where yet we thought we knew, and whence we looked forward into the present. This must be what Novalis means when he says: "Our life is not a dream; but it may become a dream, and perhaps ought to become one."

And so I looked back upon the strange history of my past; sometimes asking myself, "Can it be that all this really happened to the same *me*, who am now thinking about it in doubt and wonder?"

CHAPTER 4

Hilton Hall

As my father accompanied me to the door, where the gig, which was to carry me over the first stage of my journey, was in waiting, a large target of hide, well studded with brass nails, which had hung in the hall for time unknown—to me, at least—fell on the floor with a dull bang. My father started, but said nothing; and, as it seemed to me, rather pressed my departure than otherwise. I would have replaced the old piece of armour before I went, but he would not allow me to touch it, saying, with a grim smile,

"Take that for an omen, my boy, that your armour must be worn over the conscience, and not over the body. Be a man, Duncan, my boy. Fear nothing, and do your duty."

A grasp of the hand was all the good-bye I could

make; and I was soon rattling away to meet the coach for Edinburgh and London. Seated on the top, I was soon buried in a reverie, from which I was suddenly startled by the sound of tinkling iron. Could it be that my adversary was riding unseen alongside of the coach? Was that the clank of the ominous shoe? But I soon discovered the cause of the sound, and laughed at my own apprehensiveness. For I observed that the sound was repeated every time that we passed any trees by the wayside, and that it was the peculiar echo they gave of the loose chain and steel work about the harness. The sound was quite different from that thrown back by the houses on the road. I became perfectly familiar with it before the day was over.

I reached London in safety, and slept at the house of an old friend of my father, who treated me with great kindness, and seemed altogether to take a liking to me. Before I left he held out a hope of being able, some day or other, to procure for me what I so much desired—a commission in the army.

After spending a day or two with him, and seeing something of London, I climbed once more on the roof of a coach; and, late in the afternoon, was set down at the great gate of Hilton Hall. I walked up the broad avenue, through the final arch of which, as through a huge Gothic window, I saw the hall in the distance. Everything about me looked strange, rich, and lovely. Accustomed to the scanty flowers and diminutive wood of my own country, what I now saw gave me a feeling of majestic plenty, which I can recall at will, but which I have never experienced again. Behind the trees which formed the avenue, I saw a shrubbery, composed entirely of flowering

plants, almost all unknown to me. Issuing from the avenue, I found myself amid open, wide, lawny spaces, in
which the flower-beds lay like islands of colour. A statue
on a pedestal, the only white thing in the surrounding
green, caught my eye. I had seen scarcely any sculpture;
and this, attracting my attention by a favourite contrast
of colour, retained it by its own beauty. It was a Dryad,
or some nymph of the woods, who had just glided from
the solitude of the trees behind, and had sprung upon
the pedestal to look wonderingly around her. A few large
brown leaves lay at her feet, borne thither by some eddy-
ing wind from the trees behind. As I gazed, filled with a
new pleasure, a drop of rain upon my face made me look
up. From a grey, fleecy cloud, with sun-whitened border,
a light, gracious, plentiful rain was falling. A rainbow
sprang across the sky, and the statue stood within the
rainbow. At the same moment, from the base of the
pedestal rose a figure in white, graceful as the Dryad
above, and neither running, nor appearing to walk
quickly, yet fleet as a ghost, glided past me at a few paces'
distance, and, keeping in a straight line for the main
entrance of the hall, entered by it and vanished.

I followed in the direction of the mansion, which was
large, and of several styles and ages. One wing appeared
especially ancient. It was neglected and out of repair, and
had in consequence a desolate, almost sepulchral look,
an expression heightened by the number of large cy-
presses which grew along its line. I went up to the central
door and knocked. It was opened by a grave, elderly
butler. I passed under its flat arch, as if into the midst of
the waiting events of my story. For, as I glanced around
the hall, my consciousness was suddenly saturated, if I

may be allowed the expression, with the strange feeling
—known to every one, and yet so strange—that I had
seen it before; that, in fact, I knew it perfectly. But what
was yet more strange, and far more uncommon, was,
that, although the feeling with regard to the hall faded
and vanished instantly, and although I could not in the
least surmise the appearance of any of the regions into
which I was about to be ushered, I yet followed the butler
with a kind of indefinable expectation of seeing something which I had seen before; and every room or passage in that mansion affected me, on entering it for the
first time, with the same sensation of previous acquaintance which I had experienced with regard to the hall.
This sensation, in every case, died away at once, leaving
that portion such as it might be expected to look to one
who had never before entered the place.

I was received by the housekeeper, a little, prim, be-
nevolent old lady, with colourless face and antique head-
dress, who led me to the room prepared for me. To my
surprise, I found a large wood-fire burning on the
hearth; but the feeling of the place revealed at once the
necessity for it; and I scarcely needed to be informed that
the room, which was upon the ground floor, and looked
out upon a little solitary grass-grown and ivy-mantled
court, had not been used for years, and therefore required to be thus prepared for an inmate. My bedroom
was a few paces down a passage to the right.

Left alone, I proceeded to make a more critical survey
of my room. Its look of ancient mystery was to me incom-
parably more attractive than any show of elegance or
comfort could have been. It was large and low, panelled

throughout in oak, black with age, and worm-eaten in many parts—otherwise entire. Both the windows looked into the little court or yard before mentioned. All the heavier furniture of the room was likewise of black oak, but the chairs and couches were covered with faded tapestry and tarnished gilding, apparently the superannuated members of the general household of seats. I could give an individual description of each, for every atom in that room, large enough for discernable shape or colour, seems branded into my brain. If I happen to have the least feverishness on me, the moment I fall asleep, I am in that room.

CHAPTER 5

Lady Alice

WHEN the bell rang for dinner, I managed to find
my way to the drawing-room, where were assembled
Lady Hilton, her only daughter, a girl of about thirteen, and the two boys, my pupils. Lady Hilton would
have been pleasant, could she have been as natural as
she wished to appear. She received me with some degree of kindness; but the half-cordiality of her manner
towards me was evidently founded on the impassable-
ness of the gulf between us. I knew at once that we
should never be friends; that she would never come
down from the lofty table-land upon which she
walked; and that if, after being years in the house, I
should happen to be dying, she would send the
housekeeper to me. All right, no doubt; I only say
that it was so. She introduced to me my pupils; fine,

open-eyed, manly English boys, with something a little overbearing in their manner, which speedily disappeared in relation to me. Lord Hilton was not at home. Lady Hilton led the way to the dining-room; the elder boy gave his arm to his sister, and I was about to follow with the younger, when from one of the deep bay windows glided out, still in white, the same figure which had passed me upon the lawn. I started, and drew back. With a slight bow, she preceded me, and followed the others down the great staircase. Seated at table, I had leisure to make my observations upon them all; but most of my glances found their way to the lady who, twice that day, had affected me like an apparition. What is time, but the airy ocean in which ghosts come and go!

She was about twenty years of age; rather above the middle height, and rather slight in form; her complexion white rather than pale, her face being only less white than the deep marbly whiteness of her arms. Her eyes were large, and full of liquid night—a night throbbing with the light of invisible stars. Her hair seemed raven-black, and in quantity profuse. The expression of her face, however, generally partook more of vagueness than any other characteristic. Lady Hilton called her Lady Alice; and she never addressed Lady Hilton but in the same ceremonious style.

I afterwards learned from the old housekeeper, that Lady Alice's position in the family was a very peculiar one. Distantly connected with Lord Hilton's family on the mother's side, she was the daughter of the late Lord Glendarroch, and stepdaughter to Lady Hilton, who had

become Lady Hilton within a year after Lord Glendarroch's death. Lady Alice, then quite a child, had accompanied her stepmother, to whom she was moderately
attached, and who had been allowed to retain undis-
puted possession of her. She had no near relatives, else
the fortune I afterwards found to be at her disposal
would have aroused contending claims to the right of
guardianship.

Although she was in many respects kindly treated by
her stepmother, certain peculiarities tended to her isolation from the family pursuits and pleasures. Lady Alice
had no accomplishments. She could neither spell her
own language, nor even read it aloud. Yet she delighted
in reading to herself, though, for the most part, books
which Mrs. Wilson characterised as very odd. Her voice,
when she spoke, had a quite indescribable music in it; yet
she neither sang nor played. Her habitual motion was
more like a rhythmical gliding than an ordinary walk, yet
she could not dance. Mrs. Wilson hinted at other and
more serious peculiarities, which she either could not, or
would not describe; always shaking her head gravely and
sadly, and becoming quite silent, when I pressed for
further explanation; so that, at last, I gave up all attempts
to arrive at an understanding of the mystery by her
means. Not the less, however, I speculated on the sub-
ject.

One thing soon became evident to me: that she was
considered not merely deficient as to the power of intellectual acquirement, but in a quite abnormal intellectual
condition. Of this, however, I could myself see no sign.
The peculiarity, almost oddity, of some of her remarks,

was evidently not only misunderstood, but, with relation to her mental state, misinterpreted. Such remarks Lady Hilton generally answered only by an elongation of the lips intended to represent a smile. To me, they appeared to indicate a nature closely allied to genius, if not identical with it—a power of regarding things from an original point of view, which perhaps was the more unfettered in its operation from the fact that she was incapable of looking at them in the ordinary commonplace way. It seemed to me, sometimes, as if her point of observation was outside of the sphere within which the thing observed took place; and as if what she said, had a relation, occasionally, to things and thoughts and mental conditions familiar to her, but at which not even a definite guess could be made by me. I am compelled to acknowledge, however, that with such utterances as these mingled now and then others, silly enough for any drawing-room young lady; which seemed again to be accepted by the family as proofs that she was not *altogether* out of her right mind. She was gentle and kind to the children, as they were still called; and they seemed reasonably fond of her.

There was something to me exceedingly touching in the solitariness of this girl; for no one spoke to her as if she were like other people, or as if any heartiness were possible between them. Perhaps no one could have felt quite at home with her but a mother, whose heart had been one with hers from a season long anterior to the development of any repulsive oddity. But her position was one of peculiar isolation, for no one really approached her individual being; and that she should be unaware of this loneliness, seemed to me saddest of all. I soon found, however, that the most distant attempt on my part to show her attention, was either received with absolute indifference, or coldly repelled without the slightest acknowledgment.

But I return to the first night of my sojourn at Hilton Hall.

CHAPTER 6

My Quarters

AFTER making arrangements for commencing work in the morning, I took my leave, and retired to my own room, intent upon carrying out with more minuteness the survey I had already commenced: several cupboards in the wall, and one or two doors, apparently of closets, had especially attracted my attention. Strange was its look as I entered—as of a room hollowed out of the past, for a memorial of dead times. The fire had sunk low, and lay smouldering beneath the white ashes, like the life of the world beneath the snow, or the heart of a man beneath cold and grey thoughts. I lighted the candles which stood upon the table, but the room, instead of being brightened, looked blacker than before, for the light revealed its essential blackness.

As I cast my eyes around me, standing with my

back to the hearth (on which, for mere companion-
ship's sake, I had just heaped fresh wood), a thrill ran
suddenly throughout my frame. I felt as if, did it last
a moment longer, I should become aware of another
presence in the room; but, happily for me, it ceased
before it had reached that point; and I, recovering my
courage, remained ignorant of the cause of my fear, if
there were any, other than the nature of the room itself. With a candle in my hand, I proceeded to open
the various cupboards and closets. At first I found
nothing remarkable about any of them. The latter
were quite empty, except the last I came to, which
had a piece of very old elaborate tapestry hanging at
the back of it. Lifting this up, I saw what seemed at
first to be panels, corresponding to those which
formed the room; but on looking more closely, I discovered that this back of the closet was, or had been,
a door. There was nothing unusual in this, especially
in such an old house; but the discovery roused in me
a strong desire to know what lay behind the old door.
I found that it was secured only by an ordinary bolt,
from which the handle had been removed. Soothing
my conscience with the reflection that I had a right to
know what sort of place had communication with my
room, I succeeded, by the help of my deer-knife, in
forcing back the rusty bolt; and though, from the stiff-
ness of the hinges, I dreaded a crack, they yielded at
last with only a creak.

The opening door revealed a large hall, empty utterly,
save of dust and cobwebs, which festooned it in all quarters, and gave it an appearance of unutterable desola-

tion. The now familiar feeling, that I had seen the place before, filled my mind the first moment, and passed away the next. A broad, right-angled staircase, with massive banisters, rose from the middle of the hall. This staircase could not have originally belonged to the ancient wing which I had observed on my first approach, being much more modern; but I was convinced, from the observations I had made as to the situation of my room, that I was bordering upon, if not within, the oldest portion of the pile. In sudden horror, lest I should hear a light footfall upon the awful stair, I withdrew hurriedly, and having secured both the doors, betook myself to my bedroom; in whose dingy fourpost bed, with its carving and plumes reminding me of a hearse, I was soon ensconced amidst the snowiest linen, with the sweet and clean odour of lavender. In spite of novelty, antiquity, speculation, and dread, I was soon fast asleep; becoming thereby a fitter inhabitant of such regions, than when I moved about with restless and disturbing curiosity, through their ancient and deathlike repose.

I made no use of my discovered door, although I always intended doing so; especially after, in talking about the building with Lady Hilton, I found that I was at perfect liberty to make what excursions I pleased into the deserted portions.

My pupils turned out to be teachable, and therefore my occupation was pleasant. Their sister frequently came to me for help, as there happened to be just then an interregnum of governesses: soon she settled into a regular pupil.

After a few weeks Lord Hilton returned. Though my

room was so far from the great hall, I heard the clank of his spurs on its pavement. I trembled; for it sounded like the broken shoe. But I shook off the influence in a moment, heartily ashamed of its power over me. Soon I became familiar enough both with the sound and its cause; for his lordship rarely went anywhere except on horseback, and was booted and spurred from morning till night.

He received me with some appearance of interest, which immediately stiffened and froze. Beginning to shake hands with me as if he meant it, he instantly dropped my hand, as if it had stung him.

His nobility was of that sort which stands in constant need of repair. Like a weakly constitution, it required keeping up, and his lordship could not be said to neglect it; for he seemed to find his principal employment in administering continuous doses of obsequiousness to his own pride. His rank, like a coat made for some large ancestor, hung loose upon him: he was always trying to persuade himself that it was an excellent fit, but ever with an unacknowledged misgiving. This misgiving might have done him good, had he not met it with renewed efforts at looking that which he feared he was not. Yet this man was capable of the utmost persistency in carrying out any scheme he had once devised. Enough of him for the present: I seldom came into contact with him.

I scarcely ever saw Lady Alice, except at dinner, or by accidental meeting in the grounds and passages of the house; and then she took no notice of me whatever.

CHAPTER 7

The Library

ONE day, a week after his arrival, Lord Hilton gave a dinner-party to some of his neighbours and tenants. I entered the drawing-room rather late, and saw that, though there were many guests, not one was talking to Lady Alice. She appeared, however, altogether unconscious of neglect. Presently dinner was announced, and the company marshalled themselves, and took their way to the dining-room. Lady Alice was left unattended, the guests taking their cue from the behaviour of their entertainers. I ventured to go up to her, and offer her my arm. She made me a haughty bow, and passed on before me unaccompanied. I could not help feeling hurt at this, and I think she saw it; but it made no difference to her behaviour, except that she avoided everything that might occasion me the chance of offering my services.

Nor did I get any further with Lady Hilton. Her manner and smile remained precisely the same as on our first interview. She did not even show any interest in the fact that her daughter, Lady Lucy, had joined her brothers in the schoolroom. I had an uncomfortable feeling that the latter was like her mother, and was not to be trusted. Self-love is the foulest of all foul feeders, and will defile that it may devour. But I must not anticipate.

The neglected library was open to me at all hours; and in it I often took refuge from the dreariness of unsympathetic society. I was never admitted within the magic circle of the family interests and enjoyments. If there was such a circle, Lady Alice and I certainly stood outside of it; but whether even then it had any real inside to it, I doubted much. Nevertheless, as I have said, our common exclusion had not the effect of bringing us together as sharers of the same misfortune. In the library I found companions more to my need. But, even there, they were not easy to find; for the books were in great confusion. I could discover no catalogue, nor could I hear of the existence of such a useless luxury. One morning at breakfast, therefore, I asked Lord Hilton if I might arrange and catalogue the books during my leisure hours. He replied,

"Do anything you like with them, Mr. Campbell, except destroy them."

Now I was in my element. I never had been by any means a book-worm; but the very outside of a book had a charm to me. It was a kind of sacrament—an outward and visible sign of an inward and spiritual grace; as, indeed, what on God's earth is not? So I set to work amongst the books, and soon became familiar with many titles at least, which had been perfectly unknown to me before. I found a perfect set of our poets—perfect according to the notion of the editor and the issue of the publisher, although it omitted both Chaucer and George Herbert. I began to nibble at that portion of the collection which belonged to the sixteenth century; but with little success. I found nothing, to my idea, but love poems without any love in them, and so I soon became weary. But I found in the library what I liked far better —many romances of a very marvellous sort, and plentiful interruption they gave to the formation of the catalogue. I likewise came upon a whole nest of the German classics, which seemed to have kept their places undisturbed, in virtue of their unintelligibility. There must have been some well-read scholar in the family, and that not long before, to judge by the near approach of the line of this literature; happening to be a tolerable reader of German, I found in these volumes a mine of wealth inexhaustible. I learned from Mrs. Wilson that this scholar was a younger brother of Lord Hilton, who had died about twenty years before. He had led a retired, rather lonely life, was of a melancholy and brooding disposition, and was reported to have had an unfortunate love-story. This was one of many histories which she gave me. For the library being dusty as a catacomb, the private room of Old Time himself, I had often to betake myself to her for assistance. The good lady had far more regard than the owners of it for the library, and was delighted with the pains I was taking to rearrange and clean it. She would allow no one to help me but herself; and to many a

long-winded story, most of which I forgot as soon as I
heard them, did I listen, or seem to listen, while she
dusted the shelves and I the books.

One day I had sent a servant to ask Mrs. Wilson to
come to me. I had taken down all the books from a
hitherto undisturbed corner, and had seated myself on
a heap of them, no doubt a very impersonation of the
genius of the place; for while I waited for the
housekeeper, I was consuming a morsel of an ancient
metrical romance. After waiting for some time, I glanced
towards the door, for I had begun to get impatient for
the entrance of my helper. To my surprise, there stood
Lady Alice, her eyes fixed upon me with an expression
I could not comprehend. Her face instantly altered to its
usual look of indifference, dashed with the least possible
degree of scorn, as she turned and walked slowly away.
I rose involuntarily. An old cavalry sword, which I had
just taken down from the wall, and had placed leaning
against the books from which I now rose, fell with a clash
to the floor. I started; for it was a sound that always
startled me; and stooping I lifted the weapon. But what
was my surprise when I raised my head, to see once more
the face of Lady Alice staring in at the door! yet not the
same face, for it had changed in the moment that had
passed. It was pale with fear—not fright; and her great
black eyes were staring beyond me as if she saw something through the wall of the room. Once more her face
altered to the former scornful indifference, and she vanished. Keen of hearing as I was, I had never yet heard the
footstep of Lady Alice.

CHAPTER 8

The Somnambulist

ONE night I was sitting in my room, devouring an old romance which I had brought from the library. It was late. The fire blazed bright; but the candles were nearly burnt out, and I grew sleepy over the volume, romance as it was.

Suddenly I found myself on my feet, listening with an agony of intention. Whether I had heard anything I could not tell; but I felt as if I had. Yes; I was sure of it. Far away, somewhere in the labyrinthine pile, I heard a faint cry. Driven by some secret impulse, I flew, without a moment's reflection, to the closet door, lifted the tapestry within, unfastened the second door, and stood in the great waste echoing hall, amid the touches, light and ghostly, of the cobwebs set afloat in the eddies occasioned by my sudden entrance.

A faded moonbeam fell on the floor, and filled the
place with an ancient dream-light, which wrought
strangely on my brain, and filled it, as if it, too, were but
a deserted, sleepy house, haunted by old dreams and
memories. Recollecting myself, I went back for a light;
but the candles were both flickering in the sockets, and
I was compelled to trust to the moon. I ascended the
staircase. Old as it was, not a board creaked, not a banis-
ter shook—the whole felt solid as rock. Finding, at
length, no more stair to ascend, I groped my way on; for
here there was no direct light from the moon—only the
light of the moonlit air. I was in some trepidation, I
confess; for how should I find my way back? But the
worst result likely to ensue was, that I should have to
spend the night without knowing where; for with the first
glimmer of morning, I should be able to return to my
room. At length, after wandering into several rooms and
out again, my hand fell on a latched door. I opened it,
and entered a long corridor, with many windows on one
side. Broad strips of moonlight lay slantingly across the
narrow floor, divided by regular intervals of shade.

I started, and my heart swelled; for I saw a movement
somewhere—I could neither tell where, nor of what: I
was only aware of motion. I stood in the first shadow, and
gazed, but saw nothing. I sped across the light to the next
shadow, and stood again, looking with fearful fixedness
of gaze towards the far end of the corridor. Suddenly a
white form glimmered and vanished. I crossed to the
next shadow. Again a glimmer and vanishing, but nearer.
Nerving myself to the utmost, I ceased the stealthiness
of my movements, and went forward, slowly and steadily.

A tall form, apparently of a woman dressed in a long white robe, appeared in one of the streams of light, threw its arms over its head, gave a wild cry—which, notwithstanding its wildness and force, had a muffled sound, as if many folds, either of matter or of space, intervened— and fell at full length along the moonlight. Amidst the thrill of agony which shook me at the cry, I rushed forward, and, kneeling beside the prostrate figure, discovered that, unearthly as was the scream which had preceded her fall, it was the Lady Alice. I saw the fact in a moment: the Lady Alice was a somnambulist. Startled by the noise of my advance, she had awaked; and the usual terror and fainting had followed.

She was cold and motionless as death. What was to be done? If I called, the probability was that no one would hear me; or if any one should hear—but I need not follow the course of my thought, as I tried in vain to recover the poor girl. Suffice it to say that, both for her sake and my own, I could not face the chance of being found, in the dead of night, by common-minded domestics, in such a situation.

I was kneeling by her side, not knowing what to do, when a horror, as from the presence of death suddenly recognised, fell upon me. I thought she must be dead. But at the same moment, I heard, or seemed to hear (how should I know which?), the rapid gallop of a horse, and the clank of a loose shoe.

In an agony of fear I caught her up in my arms, and, carrying her on my arms, as one carries a sleeping child, hurried back through the corridor. Her hair, which was loose, trailed on the ground; and, as I fled, I trampled on it and stumbled. She moaned; and that instant the gallop ceased. I lifted her up across my shoulder, and carried her more easily. How I found my way to the stair I cannot tell: I know that I groped about for some time, like one in a dream with a ghost in his arms. At last I reached it, and descending, crossed the hall, and entered my room. There I placed Lady Alice upon an old couch, secured the doors, and began to breathe—and think. The first thing was to get her warm, for she was cold as the dead. I covered her with my plaid and my dressing-gown, pulled the couch before the fire, and considered what to do next.

CHAPTER 9

The First Waking

WHILE I hesitated, Nature had her own way, and, with a deep-drawn sigh, Lady Alice opened her eyes. Never shall I forget the look of mingled bewilderment, alarm, and shame, with which her great eyes met mine. But, in a moment, this expression changed to that of anger. Her dark eyes flashed with light; and a cloud of roseate wrath grew in her face, till it glowed with the opaque red of a camellia. She had almost started from the couch, when, apparently discovering the unsuitableness of her dress, she checked her impetuosity, and remained leaning on her elbow. Overcome by her anger, her beauty, and my own confusion, I knelt before her, unable to speak, or to withdraw my eyes from hers. After a moment's pause, she began to question me like a queen, and I to reply like a culprit.

"How did I come here?"

"I carried you."

"Where did you find me, pray?"

Her lip curled with ten times the usual scorn.

"In the old house, in a long corridor."

"What right had you to be there?"

"I heard a cry, and could not help going."

" 'Tis impossible—I see. Some wretch told you, and you watched for me."

"I did not, Lady Alice."

She burst into tears, and fell back on the couch, with her face turned away. Then, anger reviving, she went on through her sobs,

"Why did you not leave me where I fell? You had done enough to hurt me without bringing me here."

And again she fell a-weeping.

Now I found words.

"Lady Alice," I said, "how could I leave you lying in the moonlight? Before the sun rose, the terrible moon might have distorted your beautiful face."

"Be silent, sir. What have you to do with my face?"

"And the wind, Lady Alice, was blowing through the corridor windows, keen and cold as the moonlight. How could I leave you?"

"You could have called for help."

"Forgive me, Lady Alice, if I erred in thinking you would rather command the silence of a gentleman to whom an accident had revealed your secret, than be exposed to the domestics who would have gathered round us."

Again she half raised herself, and again her eyes flashed.

"A secret with *you*, sir!"

"But, besides, Lady Alice," I cried, springing to my feet, in distress at her hardness, "I heard the horse with the clanking shoe, and, in terror, I caught you up, and fled with you, almost before I knew what I did. And I hear it now—I hear it now!" I cried, as once more the ominous sound rang through my brain.

The angry glow faded from her face, and its paleness grew almost ghastly with dismay.

"Do *you* hear it?" she said, throwing back her covering, and rising from the couch. "I do not."

She stood listening with distended eyes, as if *they* were the gates by which such sounds entered.

"I do not hear it," she said again, after a pause. "It must be gone now." Then, turning to me, she laid her hand on my arm, and looked at me. Her black hair, disordered and entangled, wandered all over her white dress to her knees. Her face was paler than ever; and her eyes were so wide open that I could see the white all round the large dark iris.

"Did you hear it?" she said. "No one ever heard it before but me. I must forgive you—you could not help it. I will trust you, too. Take me to my room."

Without a word of reply, I wrapped my plaid about her. Then bethinking me of my chamber candle, I lighted it, and opening the two doors, led her out of the room.

"How is this?" she asked. "Why do you take me this way? I do not know the place."

"This is the way I brought you in, Lady Alice," I answered. "I know no other way to the spot where I found you. And I can guide you no farther than there—hardly even so far, for I groped my way there for the first time this night or morning—whichever it may be."

"It is past midnight, but not morning yet," she replied. "I always know. But there must be another way from your room?"

"Yes, of course; but we should have to pass the housekeeper's door—she is always late."

"Are we near her room? I should know my way from there. I fear it would not surprise any of the household to see me. They would say—'It is only Lady Alice.' Yet I cannot tell you how I shrink from being seen. No—I will try the way you brought me—if you do not mind going back with me."

This conversation passed in low tone and hurried words. It was scarcely over before we found ourselves at the foot of the staircase. Lady Alice shivered, and drew the plaid close round her. We ascended, and soon found the corridor; but when we got through it, she was rather bewildered. At length, after looking into several of the rooms, empty all, except for stray articles of ancient furniture, she exclaimed, as she entered one, and, taking the candle from my hand, held it above her head,

"Ah, yes! I am right at last. This is the haunted room. I know my way now."

I caught a darkling glimpse of a large room, apparently quite furnished; but how, except from the general feeling of antiquity and mustiness, I could not tell. Little did I think then what memories—old now, like the ghosts that with them haunt the place—would ere long find their being and take their abode in that ancient room, to forsake it never more. In strange, half-waking moods, I seem to see the ghosts and the memories flitting together through the spectral moonlight, and weaving mystic dances in and out of the storeyed windows and the tapestried walls.

At the door of this room she said, "I must leave you here. I will put down the light a little farther on, and you can come for it. I owe you many thanks. You will not be afraid of being left so near the haunted room?"

I assured her that at present I felt strong enough to meet all the ghosts in or out of Hades. Turning, she smiled a sad, sweet smile, then went on a few paces, and disappeared. The light, however, remained; and I found the candle, with my plaid, deposited at the foot of a short flight of steps, at right angles to the passage she left me in. I made my way back to my room, threw myself on the couch on which she had so lately lain, and neither went to bed nor slept that night. Before the morning, I had fully entered that phase of individual development commonly called *love;* of which the real nature is as great a mystery to me now, as it was at any period previous to its evolution in myself.

CHAPTER 10

Love and Power

WHEN the morning came, I began to doubt whether my wakefulness had not been part of my dream, and I had not dreamed the whole of my supposed adventures. There was no sign of a lady's presence left in the room. How could there have been? But throwing the plaid which covered me aside, my hand was caught by a single thread of something so fine that I could not see it till the light grew strong. I wound it round and round my finger, and doubted no longer.

At breakfast there was no Lady Alice—nor at dinner. I grew uneasy, but what could I do? I soon learned that she was ill; and a weary fortnight passed before I saw her again. Mrs. Wilson told me that she had caught cold, and was confined to her room. So I was ill at ease, not from love alone, but from anxiety as well. Every night I crept up through the deserted house to the stair where she had vanished, and there sat in the darkness or groped and peered about for some sign. But I saw no light even, and did not know where her room was. It might be far beyond this extremity of my knowledge; for I discovered no indication of the proximity of the inhabited portion of the house. Mrs. Wilson said there was nothing serious the matter; but this did not satisfy me, for I imagined something mysterious in the way in which she spoke.

As the days went on, and she did not appear, my soul began to droop within me; my intellect seemed about to desert me altogether. In vain I tried to read. Nothing could fix my attention. I read and re-read the same page; but although I understood every word as I read, I found, when I came to a pause, that there lingered in my mind no palest notion of the idea. It was just what one experiences in attempting to read when half-asleep.

I tried Euclid, and fared a little better with that. But having now to initiate my boys into the mysteries of equations, I soon found that although I could manage a very simple one, yet when I attempted one more complex—one in which something bordering upon imagination was necessary to find out the object for which to appoint the symbol to handle it by—the necessary power of concentration was itself a missing factor.

But although my thoughts were thus beyond my control, my duties were not altogether irksome to me. I remembered that they kept me near her; and although I could not learn, I found that I could teach a little.

Perhaps it is foolish to dwell upon an individual variety of an almost universal stage in the fever of life; but one exception to these indications of mental paralysis I think worth mentioning.

I continued my work in the library, although it did not advance with the same steadiness as before. One day, in listless mood, I took up a volume, without knowing what it was, or what I sought. It opened at the *Amoretti* of Edmund Spenser. I was on the point of closing it again, when a line caught my eye. I read the sonnet; read another; found I could understand them perfectly; and that hour the poetry of the sixteenth century, hitherto a sealed fountain, became an open well of refreshment, and the strength that comes from sympathy. What if its second-rate writers were full of conceits and vagaries, the feelings are very indifferent to the mere intellectual forms around which the same feelings in others have gathered, if only by their means they hint at, and sometimes express themselves. Now I understood this old fantastic verse, and knew that the foam-bells on the torrent of passionate feeling are iris-hued. And what was more—it proved an intellectual nexus between my love and my studies, or at least a bridge by which I could pass from the one to the other.

That same day, I remember well, Mrs. Wilson told me that Lady Alice was much better. But as days passed, and still she did not make her appearance, my anxiety only changed its object, and I feared that it was from aversion to me that she did not join the family. But her name was never mentioned in my hearing by any of the other members of it; and her absence appeared to be to them a matter of no moment or interest.

One night, as I sat in my room, I found, as usual, that

it was impossible to read; and throwing the book aside, relapsed into that sphere of thought which now filled my soul, and had for its centre the Lady Alice. I recalled her form as she lay on the couch, and brooded over the remembrance till a longing to see her, almost unbearable, arose within me.

"Would to heaven," I said to myself, "that will were power!"

In this concurrence of idleness, distraction, and vehement desire, I found all at once, without any foregone resolution, that I was concentrating and intensifying within me, until it rose almost to a command, the operative volition that Lady Alice should come to me. In a moment more I trembled at the sense of a new power which sprang into conscious being within me. I had had no prevision of its existence when I gave way to such extravagant and apparently helpless wishes. I now actually awaited the fulfilment of my desire; but in a condition ill fitted to receive it, for the effort had already exhausted me to such a degree, that every nerve was in a conscious tremor. Nor had I long to wait.

I heard no sound of approach: the closet door folded back, and in glided, open-eyed, but sightless, pale as death, and clad in white, ghostly pure and saintlike, the Lady Alice. I shuddered from head to foot at what I had done. She was more terrible to me in that moment than any pale-eyed ghost could have been. For had I not exercised a kind of necromantic art, and roused without awaking the slumbering dead? She passed me, walking round the table at which I was seated, went to the couch, laid herself down with a maidenly care, turned a little on one side, with her face towards me, and gradually closed her eyes. In something deeper than sleep she lay, and yet not in death. I rose, and once more knelt beside her, but dared not touch her. In what far realms of life might the lovely soul be straying! What mysterious modes of being might now be the homely surroundings of her second life! Thoughts unutterable rose in me, culminated, and sank, like the stars of heaven, as I gazed on the present symbol of an absent life—a life that I loved by means of the symbol; a symbol that I loved because of the life. How long she lay thus, how long I gazed upon her thus, I do not know.

Gradually, but without my being able to distinguish the gradations, her countenance altered to that of one who sleeps. But the change did not end there. A colour, faint as the blush in the centre of a white rose, tinged her lips, and deepened; then her cheek began to share in the hue, then her brow and her neck. The colour was that of the cloud which, the farthest from the sunset, yet acknowledges the rosy atmosphere. I watched, as it were, the dawn of a soul on the horizon of the visible. The first approaches of its far-off flight were manifest; and as I watched, I saw it come nearer and nearer, till its great, silent, speeding pinions were folded, and it looked forth, a calm, beautiful, infinite woman, from the face and form sleeping before me.

I knew that she was awake, some moments before she opened her eyes. When at last those depths of darkness disclosed themselves, slowly uplifting their white cloudy portals, the same consternation she had formerly manifested, accompanied by yet greater anger, followed.

"Yet again! Am I your slave, because I am weak?" She rose in the majesty of wrath, and moved towards the door.

"Lady Alice, I have not touched you. I am to blame, but not as you think. Could I help longing to see you? And if the longing passed, ere I was aware, into a will that you should come, and you obeyed it, forgive me."

I hid my face in my hands, overcome by conflicting emotions. A kind of stupor came over me. When I lifted my head, she was standing by the closet door.

"I have waited," she said, "to make a request of you."

"Do not utter it, Lady Alice. I know what it is. I give you my word—my solemn promise, if you like—that I will never do it again." She thanked me, with a smile, and vanished.

Much to my surprise, she appeared at dinner next day. No notice was taken of her, except by the younger of my pupils, who called out,

"Hallo, Alice! Are you down?"

She smiled and nodded, but did not speak. Everything went on as usual. There was no change in her behaviour, except in one point. I ventured the experiment of paying her some ordinary enough attention. She thanked me, without a trace of the scornful expression I all but expected to see upon her beautiful face. But when I addressed her about the weather, or something equally interesting, she made no reply; and Lady Hilton gave me a stare, as much as to say, "Don't you know it's of no use to talk to her?" Alice saw the look, and colouring to the eyes, rose, and left the room. When she had gone, Lady Hilton said to me,

"Don't speak to her, Mr. Campbell—it distresses her. She is very peculiar, you know."

She could not hide the scorn and dislike with which she spoke; and I could not help saying to myself, "What a different thing scorn looks on *your* face, Lady Hilton!" for it made her positively and hatefully ugly for the moment—to my eyes, at least.

After this, Alice sat down with us at all our meals, and seemed tolerably well. But, in some indescribable way, she was quite a different person from the Lady Alice who had twice awaked in my presence. To use a phrase common in describing one of weak intellect—she never seemed to be all there. There was something automatical in her movements; and a sort of frozen indifference was the prevailing expression of her countenance. When she smiled, a sweet light shone in her eyes, and she looked for the moment like the Lady Alice of my nightly dreams. But, altogether, the Lady Alice of the night, and the Lady Alice of the day, were two distinct persons. I believed that the former was the real one.

What nights I had now, watching and striving lest unawares I should fall into the exercise of my new power! I allowed myself to think of her as much as I pleased in the daytime, or at least as much as I dared; for, when occupied with my pupils, I dreaded lest any abstraction should even hint that I had a thought to conceal. I knew that I could not hurt her then; for that only in the night did she enter that state of existence in which my will could exercise authority over her. But at night—at night —when I knew she lay there, and might be lying here; when but a thought would bring her, and that thought was fluttering its wings, ready to spring awake out of the dreams of my heart—then the struggle was fearful. And what added force to the temptation was, that to call her to me in the night seemed like calling the real immortal Alice forth from the tomb in which she wandered about all day. It was as painful to me to see her such in the day, as it was entrancing to remember her such as I had seen her in the night. What matter if her true self came forth in anger against me? What was I? It was enough for my life, I said, to look on her, such as she really was. "Bring her yet once, and tell her all—tell her how madly, hopelessly you love her. She will forgive you at least," said a voice within me. But I heard it as the voice of the tempter, and kept down the thought which might have grown to the will.

CHAPTER 11

A New Pupil

ONE day, exactly three weeks after her last visit to my room, as I was sitting with my three pupils in the schoolroom, Lady Alice entered, and began to look on the bookshelves as if she wanted some volume. After a few moments, she turned, and, approaching the table, said to me, in an abrupt, yet hesitating way,

"Mr. Campbell, I cannot spell. How am I to learn?"

I thought for a moment, and replied: "Copy a passage every day, Lady Alice, from some favourite book. Then, if you allow me, I shall be most happy to point out any mistakes you may have made."

"Thank you, Mr. Campbell, I will; but I am afraid you will despise me, when you find how badly I spell."

"There is no fear of that," I rejoined. "It is a mere peculiarity. So long as one can *think* well, spelling is altogether secondary."

"Thank you; I will try," she said, and left the room.

Next day, she brought me an old ballad, written tolerably, but in a schoolgirl's hand. She had copied the antique spelling, letter for letter.

"This is quite correct," I said; "but to copy such as this will not teach you properly; for it is very old, and consequently old-fashioned."

"Is it old? Don't we spell like that now? You see I do not know anything about it. You must set me a task, then."

This I undertook with more pleasure than I dared to show. Every day she brought me the appointed exercise, written with a steadily improving hand. To my surprise, I never found a single error in the spelling. Of course, when, advancing a step in the process, I made her write from my dictation, she did make blunders, but not so many as I had expected; and she seldom repeated one after correction.

This new association gave me many opportunities of doing more for her than merely teaching her to spell. We talked about what she copied; and I had to explain. I also told her about the writers. Soon she expressed a desire to know something of figures. We commenced arithmetic. I proposed geometry along with it, and found the latter especially fitted to her powers. One by one we included several other necessary branches; and ere long I had four around the schoolroom table—equally my pupils. Whether the attempts previously made to instruct her had been insufficient or misdirected, or whether her intellectual powers had commenced a fresh growth, I could not tell; but I leaned to the latter conclusion, especially after I began to observe that her peculiar remarks had become modified in form, though without losing any of their originality. The unearthliness of her beauty likewise disappeared, a slight colour displacing the almost marbly whiteness of her cheek.

Long before Lady Alice had made this progress, my nightly struggles began to diminish in violence. They had now entirely ceased. The temptation had left me. I felt certain that for weeks she had never walked in her sleep. She was beyond my power, and I was glad of it.

I was, of course, most careful of my behaviour during all this period. I strove to pay Lady Alice no more attention than I paid to the rest of my pupils; and I cannot help thinking that I succeeded. But now and then, in the midst of some instruction I was giving Lady Alice, I caught the eye of Lady Lucy, a sharp, common-minded girl, fixed upon one or the other of us, with an inquisitive vulgar expression, which I did not like. This made me more careful still. I watched my tones, to keep them even, and free from any expression of the feeling of which my heart was full. Sometimes, however, I could not help revealing the gratification I felt when she made some marvellous remark—marvellous, I mean, in relation to her other attainments; such a remark as a child will sometimes make, showing that he has already mastered, through his earnest simplicity, some question that has for ages perplexed the wise and the prudent. On one of these occasions, I found the cat eyes of Lady Lucy glittering on me. I turned away; not, I fear, without showing some displeasure.

Whether it was from Lady Lucy's evil report, or that the change in Lady Alice's habits and appearance had attracted the attention of Lady Hilton, I cannot tell; but one morning she appeared at the door of the study, and called her. Lady Alice rose and went, with a slight gesture of impatience. In a few minutes she returned, looking angry and determined, and resumed her seat. But whatever it was that had passed between them, it had destroyed that quiet flow of the feelings which was necessary to the working of her thoughts. In vain she tried: she could do nothing correctly. At last she burst into tears and left the room. I was almost beside myself with distress and apprehension. She did not return that day.

Next morning she entered at the usual hour, looking composed, but paler than of late, and showing signs of recent weeping. When we were all seated, and had just commenced our work, I happened to look up, and caught her eyes intently fixed on me. They dropped instantly, but without any appearance of confusion. She went on with her arithmetic, and succeeded tolerably. But this respite was to be of short duration. Lady Hilton again entered, and called her. She rose angrily, and my quick ear caught the half-uttered words, "That woman will make an idiot of me again!" She did not return; and never from that hour resumed her place in the schoolroom.

The time passed heavily. At dinner she looked proud and constrained; and spoke only in monosyllables.

For two days I scarcely saw her. But the third day, as I was busy in the library alone, she entered.

"Can I help you, Mr. Campbell?" she said.

I glanced involuntarily towards the door.

"Lady Hilton is not at home," she replied to my look,

while a curl of indignation contended with a sweet tremor of shame for the possession of her lip. "Let me help you."

"You will help me best if you sing that ballad I heard you singing just before you came in. I never heard you sing before."

"Didn't you? I don't think I ever did sing before."

"Sing it again, will you, please?"

"It is only two verses. My old Scotch nurse used to sing it when I was a little girl—oh, so long ago! I didn't know I could sing it."

She began without more ado, standing in the middle of the room, with her back towards the door.

> "Annie was dowie, an' Willie was wae:
> What can be the matter wi' siccan a twae?
> For Annie was bonnie's the first o' the day,
> An' Willie was strang an' honest an' gay.
>
> Oh! the tane had a daddy was poor an' was proud;
> An' the tither a minnie that cared for the gowd.
> They lo'ed ane anither, an' said their say—
> But the daddy an' minnie hae pairtit the twae."

Just as she finished the song, I saw the sharp eyes of Lady Lucy peeping in at the door.

"Lady Lucy is watching at the door, Lady Alice," I said.

"I don't care," she answered; but turned with a flush on her face, and stepped noiselessly to the door.

"There is no one there," she said, returning.

"There was, though," I answered.

"They want to drive me mad," she cried, and hurried from the room.

The next day but one, she came again with the same request. But she had not been a minute in the library before Lady Hilton came to the door and called her in angry tones.

"Presently," said Alice, and remained where she was.

"Do go, Lady Alice," I said. "They will send me away if you refuse."

She blushed scarlet, and went without another word. She came no more to the library.

CHAPTER 12

Confession

DAY followed day, the one the child of the other. Alice's old paleness and unearthly look began to reappear; and, strange to tell, my midnight temptation revived. After a time she ceased to dine with us again, and for days I never saw her. It was the old story of suffering with me, only more intense than before. The day was dreary, and the night stormy. "Call her," said my heart; but my conscience resisted.

I was lying on the floor of my room one midnight, with my face to the ground, when suddenly I heard a low, sweet, strange voice singing somewhere. The moment I became aware that I heard it I felt as if I had been listening to it unconsciously for some minutes past. I lay still, either charmed to stillness, or fearful of breaking the spell. As I lay, I was lapt in the folds of a waking dream.

I was in bed in a castle, on the seashore; the wind came from the sea in chill *eerie soughs,* and the waves fell with a threatful tone upon the beach, muttering many maledictions as they rushed up, and whispering cruel portents as they drew back, hissing and gurgling, through the million narrow ways of the pebbly ramparts; and I knew that a maiden in white was standing in the cold wind, by the angry sea, singing. I had a kind of dreamy belief in my dream; but, overpowered by the spell of the music, I still lay and listened. Keener and stronger, under the impulses of my will, grew the power of my hearing. At last I could distinguish the words. The ballad was *Annie of Lochroyan;* and Lady Alice was singing it. The words I heard were these—

> "Oh, gin I had a bonnie ship,
>   And men to sail wi' me,
> It's I wad gang to my true love,
>   Sin' he winna come to me.
>
> Lang stood she at her true love's door,
>   And lang tirled at the pin;
> At length up gat his fause mother,
>   Says, 'Wha's that wad be in?'
>
>   .   .   .   .
>
> Love Gregory started frae his sleep,
>   And to his mother did say:
> 'I dreamed a dream this night, mither,
>   That maks my heart right wae.
>
> 'I dreamed that Annie of Lochroyan,
>   The flower of a' her kin,
> Was standing mournin' at my door,
>   But nane wad let her in.' "

I sprang to my feet, and opened the hidden door. There she stood, white, asleep, with closed eyes, singing like a bird, only with a heartful of sad meaning in every tone. I stepped aside, without speaking, and she passed me into the room. I closed the door, and followed her. She lay already upon the couch, still and restful—already covered with my plaid. I sat down beside her, waiting; and gazed upon her in wonderment. That she was possessed of very superior intellectual powers, whatever might be the cause of their having lain dormant so long, I had already fully convinced myself; but I was not prepared to find art as well as intellect. I had already heard her sing the little song of two verses, which she had learned from her nurse. But here was a song, of her own making as to the music, so true and so potent, that, before I knew anything of the words, it had surrounded me with a dream of the place in which the scene of the ballad was laid. It did not then occur to me that, perhaps, our idiosyncrasies were such as not to require even the music of the ballad for the production of *rapport* between our minds, the brain of the one generating in the brain of the other the vision present to itself.

I sat and thought. Some obstruction in the gateways, outward, prevented her, in her waking hours, from uttering herself at all. This obstruction, damming back upon their sources the outgoings of life, threw her into this abnormal sleep. In it the impulse to utterance, still unsatisfied, so wrought within her unable, yet compliant form, that she could not rest, but rose and walked. And now, a fresh surge from the sea of her unknown being, unrepressed by the *hitherto* of the objects of sense, had burst the gates and bars, swept the obstructions from its channel, and poured from her in melodious song.

The first green lobes, at least, of these thoughts appeared above the soil of my mind, while I sat and gazed on the sleeping girl. And now I had once more the delight of watching a spirit-dawn, a soul-rise, in that lovely form. The light flushing of its pallid sky was, as before, the first sign. I dreaded the flash of lovely flame, and the outburst of regnant anger, ere I should have time to say that I was not to blame. But when, at length, the full dawn, the slow sunrise came, it was with all the gentleness of a cloudy summer morn. Never did a more celestial rosy red hang about the skirts of the level sun, than deepened and glowed upon her face, when, opening her eyes, she saw me beside her. She covered her face with her hands; and instead of the words of indignant reproach, which I dreaded to hear, she murmured behind the snowy screen: "I am glad you have broken your promise."

My heart gave a bound and was still. I grew faint with delight. "No," I said; "I have not broken my promise, Lady Alice; I have struggled nearly to madness to keep it—and I have kept it."

"I have come then of myself. Worse and worse! But it is their fault."

Tears now found their way through the repressing fingers. I could not endure to see her weep. I knelt beside her, and, while she still covered her face with her hands, I said—I do not know what I said. They were wild, and, doubtless, foolish words in themselves, but they must have been wise and true in their meaning. When I ceased, I knew that I had ceased only by the great silence around me. I was still looking at her hands. Slowly she withdrew them. It was as when the sun breaks forth on a cloudy day. The winter was over and gone; the time of the singing of birds had come. She smiled on me through her tears, and heart met heart in the light of that smile.

She rose to go at once, and I begged for no delay. I only stood with clasped hands, gazing at her. She turned at the door, and said,

"I daresay I shall come again; I am afraid I cannot help it; only mind you do not wake me."

Before I could reply, I was alone; and I felt that I must not follow her.

CHAPTER 13

Questioning

I LAID myself on the couch she had left, but not to sleep. A new pulse of life, stronger than I could bear, was throbbing within me. I dreaded a fever, lest I should talk in it, and drop the clue to my secret treasure. But the light of the morning stilled me, and a bath in ice-cold water made me strong again. Yet I felt all that day as if I were dying a delicious death, and going to a yet more exquisite life. As far as I might, however, I repressed all indications of my delight; and endeavoured, for the sake both of duty and of prudence, to be as attentive to my pupils and their studies as it was possible for man to be. This helped to keep me in my right mind. But, more than all my efforts at composure, the pain which, as far as my experience goes, invariably accompanies, and sometimes even usurps, the place of the pleasure which gave it birth, was efficacious in keeping me sane.

Night came, but brought no Lady Alice. It was a week before I saw her again. Her heart had been stilled, and she was able to sleep aright.

But seven nights after, she did come. I waited her awaking, possessed with one painful thought, which I longed to impart to her. She awoke with a smile, covered her face for a moment, but only for a moment, and then sat up. I stood before her; and the first words I spoke were,

"Lady Alice, ought I not to go?"

"No," she replied at once. "I can claim some compensation from them for the wrong they have been doing me. Do you know in what relation I stand to Lord and Lady Hilton? They are but my stepmother and her husband."

"I know that."

"Well, I have a fortune of my own, about which I never thought or cared—till—till—within the last few weeks. Lord Hilton is my guardian. Whether they made me the stupid creature I *was,* I do not know; but I believe they have represented me as far worse than I was, to keep people from making my acquaintance. They prevented my going on with my lessons, because they saw I was getting to understand things, and grow like other people; and that would not suit their purposes. It would be false delicacy in you to leave me to them, when you can make up to me for their injustice. Their behaviour to me takes away any right they had over me, and frees you from any obligation, because I am yours. Am I not?"

Once more she covered her face with her hands. I could answer only by withdrawing one of them, which I was now emboldened to keep in my own.

I was very willingly persuaded to what was so much my own desire. But whether the reasoning was quite just or not, I am not yet sure. Perhaps it might be so for her, and yet not for me: I do not know; I am a poor casuist.

She resumed, laying her other hand upon mine,

"It would be to tell the soul which you have called forth, to go back into its dark moaning cavern, and never more come out to the light of day."

How could I resist this?

A long pause ensued.

"It is strange," she said, at length, "to feel when I lie down at night, that I may awake in your presence, without knowing how. It is strange, too, that, although I should be utterly ashamed to come wittingly, I feel no confusion when I find myself here. When I feel myself coming awake, I lie for a little while with my eyes closed, wondering and hoping, and afraid to open them, lest I should find myself only in my own chamber; shrinking a little, too—just a little—from the first glance into your face."

"But when you awake, do you know nothing of what has taken place in your sleep?"

"Nothing whatever."

"Have you no vague sensations, no haunting shadows, no dim ghostly moods, seeming to belong to that condition, left?"

"None whatever."

She rose, said "Good-night," and left me.

CHAPTER 14

Jealousy

❧

AGAIN seven days passed before she revisited me. Indeed, her visits had always an interval of seven days, or a multiple of seven, between.

Since the last, a maddening jealousy had seized me. For, returning from those unknown regions into which her soul had wandered away, and where she had stayed for hours, did she not sometimes awake with a smile? How could I be sure that she did not lead two distinct existences?—that she had not some loving spirit, or man, who, like her, had for a time left the body behind—who was all in all to her in that region, and whom she forgot when she forsook it, as she forgot me when she entered it? It was a thought I could not brook. But I put aside its persistency as well as I could, till she should come again. For this I waited. I could not now endure the thought of compelling the attendance of her unconscious form; of making her body, like a living cage, transport to my presence the unresisting soul. I shrank from it as a true man would shrink from kissing the lips of a sleeping woman whom he loved, not knowing that she loved him in return.

It may well be said that to follow such a doubt was to inquire too curiously; but once the thought had begun, and grown, and been born, how was I to slay the monster, and be free of its hated presence? Was its truth not a possibility? Yet how could even she help me, for she knew nothing of the matter? How could she vouch for the unknown? What news can the serene face of the moon, ever the same to us, give of the hidden half of herself turned ever towards what seems to us but the blind abysmal darkness, which yet has its own light and its own life? All I could hope for was to see her, to tell her, to be comforted at least by her smile.

My saving angel glided blind into my room, lay down upon her bier, and awaited the resurrection. I sat and awaited mine, panting to untwine from my heart the cold death-worm that twisted around it, yet picturing to myself the glow of love on the averted face of the beautiful spirit—averted from me, and bending on a radiant companion all the light withdrawn from the lovely form beside me. That light began to return. "She is coming, she is coming," I said within me. "Back from its glowing south travels the sun of my spring, the glory of my summer." Floating slowly up from the infinite depths of her being, came the conscious woman; up—up from the realms of stillness lying deeper than the plummet of self-knowledge can sound; up from the formless, up into the known, up into the material, up to the windows that look forth on the embodied mysteries around. Her eyelids rose. One look of love all but slew my fear. When I told her my grief, she answered with a smile of pity, yet half of disdain at the thought,

"If ever I find it so, I will kill myself there, that I may go to my Hades with you. But if I am dreaming of another, how is it that I always rise in my vision and come to you? You will go crazy if you fancy such foolish things," she added, with a smile of reproof.

The spectral thought vanished, and I was free.

"Shall I tell you," she resumed, covering her face with her hands, "why I behaved so proudly to you, from the very first day you entered the house? It was because, when I passed you on the lawn, before ever you entered the house, I felt a strange, undefinable attraction towards you, which continued, although I could not account for it and would not yield to it. I was heartily annoyed at it. But you see it was of no use—here I am. That was what made me so fierce, too, when I first found myself in your room."

It was indeed long before she came to my room again.

CHAPTER 15

The Chamber of Ghosts

Bᴜᴛ now she returned once more into the usual routine of the family. I fear I was unable to repress all signs of agitation when, next day, she entered the dining-room, after we were seated, and took her customary place at the table. Her behaviour was much the same as before; but her face was very different. There was light in it now, and signs of mental movement. The smooth forehead would be occasionally wrinkled, and she would fall into moods which were evidently not of inanity, but of abstracted thought. She took especial care that our eyes should not meet. If by chance they did, instead of sinking hers, she kept them steady, and opened them wider, as if she was fixing them on nothing at all, or she raised them still higher, as if she was looking at something above me, before she allowed them to fall. But the

change in her altogether was such that it must have attracted the notice and roused the speculation of Lady
Hilton at least. For me, so well did she act her part, that
I was thrown into perplexity by it. And when day after
day passed, and the longing to speak to her grew, and
remained unsatisfied, new doubts arose. Perhaps she was
tired of me. Perhaps her new studies filled her mind with
the clear, gladsome morning light of the pure intellect,
which always throws doubt and distrust and a kind of
negation upon the moonlight of passion, mysterious,
and mingled ever with faint shadows of pain. I walked as
in an unresting sleep. Utterly as I loved her, I was yet
alarmed and distressed to find how entirely my being had
grown dependent upon her love; how little of individual,
self-existing, self-upholding life, I seemed to have left;
how little I cared for anything, save as I could associate
it with her.

I was sitting late one night in my room. I had all but
given up hope of her coming. I had, perhaps, deprived
her of the somnambulic power. I was brooding over this
possibility, when all at once I felt as if I were looking into
the haunted room. It seemed to be lighted by the moon,
shining through the stained windows. The feeling came
and went suddenly, as such visions of places generally
do; but this had an indescribable something about it
more clear and real than such resurrections of the past,
whether willed or unwilled, commonly possess; and a
great longing seized me to look into the room once
more. I rose with a sense of yielding to the irresistible,
left the room, groped my way through the hall and up the
oak staircase—I had never thought of taking a light with

me—and entered the corridor. No sooner had I entered it, than the thought sprang up in my mind—"What if she should be there!" My heart stood still for a moment, like a wounded deer, and then bounded on, with a pang in every bound. The corridor was night itself, with a dim, bluish-grey light from the windows, sufficing to mark their own spaces. I stole through it, and, without erring once, went straight to the haunted chamber. The door stood half open. I entered, and was bewildered by the dim, mysterious, dreamy loveliness upon which I gazed. The moon shone full upon the windows, and a thousand coloured lights and shadows crossed and intertwined upon the walls and floor, all so soft, and mingling, and undefined, that the brain was filled as with a flickering dance of ghostly rainbows. But I had little time to think of these; for out of the only dark corner in the room came a white figure, flitting across the chaos of lights, bedewed, besprinkled, bespattered, as she passed, with their multitudinous colours. I was speechless, motionless, with something far beyond joy. With a low moan of delight, Lady Alice sank into my arms. Then, looking up, with a light laugh—"The scales are turned, dear," she said. "You are in my power now; I brought you here. I thought I could, and I tried, for I wanted so much to see you—and you are come." She led me across the room to the place where she had been seated, and we sat side by side.

"I thought you had forgotten me," I said, "or had grown tired of me."

"Did you? That was unkind. You have made my heart so still, that, body and soul, I sleep at night."

"Then shall I never see you more?"

"We can meet here. This is the best place. No one dares come near the haunted room at night. We might even venture in the evening. Look, now, from where we are sitting, across the air, between the windows and the shadows on the floor. Do you see nothing moving?"

I looked, but could see nothing. She resumed.

"I almost fancy, sometimes, that what old stories say about this room may be true. I could fancy now that I see dim transparent forms in ancient armour, and in strange antique dresses, men and women, moving about, meeting, speaking, embracing, parting, coming and going. But I was never afraid of such beings. I am sure *these* would not, could not hurt us."

If the room was not really what it was well fitted to be —a rendezvous for the ghosts of the past—then either my imagination, becoming more active as she spoke, began to operate upon my brain, or her fancies were mysteriously communicated to me; for I was persuaded that I saw such dim undefined forms as she described, of a substance only denser than the moonlight, flitting and floating about, between the windows and the illuminated floor. Could they have been coloured shadows thrown from the stained glass upon the fine dust with which the slightest motion in such an old and neglected room must fill its atmosphere? I did not think of that then, however.

"I could persuade myself that I, too, see them," I replied. "I cannot say that I am afraid of such beings any more than you—if only they will not speak."

"Ah!" she replied, with a lengthened, meaning utterance, expressing sympathy with what I said; "I know what you mean. I, too, am afraid of hearing things. And that reminds me, I have never yet asked you about the galloping horse. I too hear sometimes the sound of a loose horseshoe. It always betokens some evil to me; but I do not know what it means. Do you?"

"Do you know," I rejoined, "that there is a connection between your family and mine, somewhere far back in their histories?"

"No! Is there? How glad I am! Then perhaps you and I are related, and that is how we are so much alike, and have power over each other, and hear the same things."

"Yes. I suppose that is how."

"But can you account for that sound which we both hear?"

"I will tell you what my old foster-mother told me," I replied. And I began by narrating when and where I had first heard the sound; and then gave her, as nearly as I could, the legend which nurse had recounted to me. I did not tell her its association with the events of my birth, for I feared exciting her imagination too much. She listened to it very quietly, however, and when I came to a close, only said,

"Of course, we cannot tell how much of it is true, but there may be something in it. I have never heard anything of the sort, and I, too, have an old nurse. She is with me still. You shall see her some day."

She rose to go.

"Will you meet me here again soon?" I said.

"As soon as you wish," she answered.

"Then to-morrow, at midnight?"

"Yes."

And we parted at the door of the haunted chamber. I watched the flickering with which her whiteness just set the darkness in motion, and nothing more, seeming to see it long after I knew she must have turned aside and descended the steps leading towards her own room. Then I turned and groped my way back to mine.

We often met after this in the haunted room. Indeed my spirit haunted it all day and all night long. And when we met amid the shadows, we were wrapped in the mantle of love, and from its folds looked out fearless on the ghostly world about us. Ghosts or none, they never annoyed us. Our love was a talisman, yea, an elixir of life, which made us equal to the twice-born—the disembodied dead. And they were as a wall of fear about us, to keep far off the unfriendly foot and the prying eye.

In the griefs that followed, I often thought with myself that I would gladly die for a thousand years, might I then awake for one night in the haunted chamber, a ghost, among the ghosts who crowded its stained moonbeams, and see my dead Alice smiling across the glimmering rays, and beckoning me to the old nook, she, too, having come awake out of the sleep of death, in the dream of the haunted chamber. "Might we but sit there," I said, "through the night, as of old, and love and comfort each other, till the moon go down, and the pale dawn, which is the night of the ghosts, begin to arise, then gladly would I go to sleep for another thousand years, in the hope that when I next became conscious of life, it might be in another such ghostly night, in the chamber of the ghosts."

CHAPTER 16

The Clanking Shoe

TIME passed. We began to feel very secure in that room, watched as it was by the sleepless sentry, Fear. One night I ventured to take a light with me.

"How nice to have a candle!" she said as I entered. "I hope they are all in bed, though. It will drive some of them into fits if they see the light."

"I wanted to show you something I found in the library to-day."

"What is it?"

I opened a book, and showed her a paper inside it, with some verses written on it.

"Whose writing is that?" I asked.

"Yours, of course. As if I did not know your writing!"

"Will you look at the date?"

"*Seventeen hundred and ninety-three!* You are making

game of me, Duncan. But the paper does look yellow and old."

"I found it as you see it, in that book. It belonged to Lord Hilton's brother. The verses are a translation of part of the poem beside which they lie—one by von Salis, who died shortly before that date at the bottom. I will read them to you, and then show you something else that is strange about them. The poem is called *Psyche's Sorrow. Psyche* means the soul, Alice."

"I remember. You told me about her before, you know."

"Psyche's sighing all her prison darkens;
 She is moaning for the far-off stars;
Fearing, hoping, every sound she hearkens—
 Fate may now be breaking at her bars.

Bound, fast bound, are Psyche's airy pinions:
 High her heart, her mourning soft and low—
Knowing that in sultry pain's dominions
 Grow the palms that crown the victor's brow;

That the empty hand the wreath encloses;
 Earth's cold winds but make the spirit brave;
Knowing that the briars bear the roses,
 Golden flowers the waste deserted grave.

In the cypress-shade her myrtle groweth;
 Much she loves, because she much hath borne;
Love-led, through the darksome way she goeth—
 On to meet him in the breaking morn.

She can bear—"

"Here the translation ceases, you see; and then follows the date, with the words in German underneath it 'How weary I am!' Now what is strange, Alice, is, that this date is the very month and year in which I was born.''

She did not reply to this with anything beyond a mere assent. Her mind was fixed on the poem itself. She began to talk about it, and I was surprised to find how thoroughly she entered into it and understood it. She seemed to have crowded the growth of a lifetime into the last few months. At length I told her how unhappy I had felt for some time, at remaining in Lord Hilton's house, as matters now were.

"Then you must go," she said, quite calmly.

This troubled me.

"You do not mind it?"

"No. I shall be very glad."

"Will you go with me?" I asked, perplexed.

"Of course I will."

I did not know what to say to this, for I had no money, and of course I should have none of my salary. She divined at once the cause of my hesitation.

"I have a diamond bracelet in my room," she said, with a smile, "and a few guineas besides."

"How shall we get away?"

"Nothing is easier. My old nurse, whom I mentioned to you before, lives at the lodge gate."

"Oh! I know her very well," I interrupted. "But she's not Scotch?"

"Indeed she is. But she has been with our family almost all her life. I often go to see her, and sometimes stay all night with her. You can get a carriage ready in the village, and neither of us will be missed before morning."

I looked at her in renewed surprise at the decision of

her invention. She covered her face, as she seldom did now, but went on,

"We can go to London, where you will easily find something to do. Men always can there. And when I come of age—"

"Alice, how old are you?" I interrupted.

"Nineteen," she answered. "By the way," she resumed, "when I think of it—how odd!—that"—pointing to the date on the paper—"is the very month in which I too was born."

I was too much surprised to interrupt her, and she continued,

"I never think of my age without recalling one thing about my birth, which nurse often refers to. She was going up the stair to my mother's room, when she happened to notice a bright star, not far from the new moon. As she crossed the room with me in her arms, just after I was born, she saw the same star almost on the tip of the opposite horn. My mother died a week after. Who knows how different I might have been if she had lived!"

It was long before I spoke. The awful and mysterious thoughts roused in my mind by the revelations of the day held me silent. At length I said, half thinking aloud,

"Then you and I, Alice, were born the same hour, and our mothers died together."

Receiving no answer, I looked at her. She was fast asleep, and breathing gentle, full breaths. She had been sitting for some time with her head lying on my shoulder and my arm around her. I could not bear to wake her.

We had been in this position perhaps for half an hour, when suddenly a cold shiver ran through me, and all at once I became aware of the far-off gallop of a horse. It drew dearer. On and on it came—nearer and nearer. Then came the clank of the broken shoe!

At the same moment, Alice started from her sleep and, springing to her feet, stood an instant listening. Then crying out, in an agonised whisper, "The horse with the clanking shoe!" she flung her arms around me. Her face was white as the spectral moon which, the moment I put the candle out, looked in through a clear pane beside us; and she gazed fearfully, yet wildly defiant, towards the door. We clung to each other. We heard the sound come nearer and nearer, till it thundered right up to the very door of the room, terribly loud. It ceased. But the door was flung open, and Lord Hilton entered, followed by servants with lights.

I have but a very confused remembrance of what followed. I heard a vile word from the lips of Lord Hilton; I felt my fingers on his throat; I received a blow on the head; and I seem to remember a cry of agony from Alice as I fell. What happened next I do not know.

When I came to myself, I was lying on a wide moor, with the night wind blowing about me. I presume that I had wandered thither in a state of unconsciousness, after being turned out of the Hall, and that I had at last fainted from loss of blood. I was unable to move for a long time. At length the morning broke, and I found myself not far from the Hall. I crept back, a mile or two, to the gates, and having succeeded in rousing Alice's old nurse, was taken in with many lamentations, and put to bed in the lodge. I had a violent fever; and it was all the poor woman could do to keep my presence a secret from the family at the Hall.

When I began to mend, my first question was about Alice. I learned, though with some difficulty—for my kind attendant was evidently unwilling to tell me all the truth—that Alice, too, had been very ill; and that, a week before, they had removed her. But she either would not or could not tell me where they had taken her. I believe she could not. Nor do I know for certain to this day.

Mrs. Blakesley offered me the loan of some of her savings to get me to London. I received it with gratitude, and as soon as I was fit to travel made my way thither. Afraid for my reason, if I had no employment to keep my thoughts from brooding on my helplessness, and so increasing my despair, and determined likewise that my failure should not make me burdensome to any one else, I enlisted in the Scots Greys, before letting any of my friends know where I was. Through the help of one already mentioned in my story, I soon obtained a commission. From the field of Waterloo, I rode into Brussels with a broken arm and a sabre-cut in the head.

As we passed along one of the streets, through all the clang of iron-shod hoofs on the stones around me, I heard the ominous clank. At the same moment, I heard a cry. It was the voice of my Alice. I looked up. At a barred window I saw her face; but it was terribly changed. I dropped from my horse. As soon as I was able to move from the hospital, I went to the place, and found it was a lunatic asylum. I was permitted to see the inmates, but discovered no one resembling her. I do not now believe that she was ever there. But I may be wrong. Nor will I trouble my reader with the theories on which I sought to account for the vision. They will occur to himself readily enough.

For years and years I knew not whether she was alive or dead. I sought her far and near. I wandered over England, France, and Germany, hopelessly searching; listening at tables d'hôte; lurking about mad-houses; haunting theatres and churches; often, in wild regions, begging my way from house to house; I did not find her.

Once I visited Hilton Hall. I found it all but deserted. I learned that Mrs. Wilson was dead, and that there were only two or three servants in the place. I managed to get into the house unseen, and made my way to the haunted chamber. My feelings were not so keen as I had anticipated, for they had been dulled by long suffering. But again I saw the moon shine through those windows of stained glass. Again her beams were crowded with ghosts. *She* was not amongst them. "My lost love!" I cried; and then, rebuking myself, "No; she is not lost. They say that Time and Space exist not, save in our thoughts. If so, then that which has been is, and the Past can never cease. She is mine, and I shall find her—what matters it where, or when, or how? Till then, my soul is but a moon-lighted chamber of ghosts; and I sit within, the dreariest of them all. When she enters, it will be a home of love. And I wait—I wait."

I sat and brooded over the Past, till I fell asleep in the phantom-peopled night. And all the night long they were about me—the men and women of the long past. And I was one of them. I wandered in my dreams over the whole house, habited in a long old-fashioned gown, searching for one who was Alice, and yet would be some one else. From room to room I wandered till weary, and could not find her. At last I gave up the search, and, retreating to the library, shut myself in. There, taking down from the shelf the volume of von Salis, I tried hard to go on with the translation of *Pysche's Sorrow,* from the point where the student had left it, thinking it, all the time, my own unfinished work.

When I woke in the morning, the chamber of ghosts, in which I had fallen asleep, had vanished. The sun shone in through the windows of the library; and on its dusty table lay von Salis, open at *Pysche's Trauer.* The sheet of paper with the translation on it was not there. I hastened to leave the house, and effected my escape before the servants were astir.

Sometimes I condensed my whole being into a single intensity of will—that she should come to me; and sustained it until I fainted with the effort. She did not come. I desisted altogether at last, for I bethought me that, whether dead or alive, it must cause her torture not to be able to obey it.

Sometimes I questioned my own sanity. But the thought of the loss of my reason did not in itself trouble me much. What tortured me almost to the madness it supposed was the possible fact, which a return to my right mind might reveal—that there never had been a Lady Alice. What if I died, and awoke from my madness, and found a clear blue air of life, a joyous world of sunshine, a divine wealth of delight around and in me—

but no Lady Alice—she having vanished with all the other phantoms of a sick brain! "Rather let me be mad still," I said, "if mad I am; and so dream on that I have been blessed. Were I to wake to such a heaven, I would pray God to let me go and live the life I had but dreamed, with all its sorrows, and all its despair, and all its madness; that, when I died again, I might know that such things had been, and could never be awaked from, and left behind with the dream." But I was not mad, any more than Hamlet; though, like him, despair sometimes led me far along the way at the end of which madness lies.

CHAPTER 17

The Physician

⌇⌇

I WAS now Captain Campbell, of the Scots Greys, contriving to live on my half pay, and thinking far more about the past than the present or the future. My father was dead. My only brother was also gone, and the property had passed into other hands. I had no fixed place of abode, but went from one spot to another, as the whim seized me—sometimes remaining months, sometimes removing next day, but generally choosing retired villages about which I knew nothing.

I had spent a week in a small town on the borders of Wales, and intended remaining a fortnight longer, when I was suddenly seized with a violent illness, in which I lay insensible for three weeks. When I recovered consciousness, I found that my head had been shaved, and that the cicatrice of my old wound was occasionally very painful.

Of late I have suspected that I had some operation performed upon my skull during my illness; but Dr. Ruthwell never dropped a hint to that effect. This was the friend whom, when first I opened my seeing eyes, I beheld sitting by my bedside, watching the effect of his last prescription. He was one of the few in the profession, whose love of science and love of their fellows combined would be enough to chain them to the art of healing, irrespective of its emoluments. He was one of the few, also, who see the marvellous in all science, and, therefore, reject nothing merely because the marvellous may seem to predominate in it. Yet neither would he accept anything of the sort as fact, without the strictest use of every experiment within his power, even then remaining often in doubt. This man conferred honour by his friendship; and I am happy to think that before many days of recovery had passed, we were friends indeed. But I lay for months under his care before I was able to leave my bed.

He attributed my illness to the consequences of the sabre-cut, and my recovery to the potency of the drugs he had exhibited. I attributed my illness in great measure to the constant contemplation of my early history, no longer checked by any regular employment; and my recovery in equal measure to the power of his kindness and sympathy, helping from within what could never have been reached from without.

He told me that he had often been greatly perplexed with my symptoms, which would suddenly change in the most unaccountable manner, exhibiting phases which did not, as far as his knowledge went, belong to any variety of the suffering which gave the prevailing character to my ailment; and after I had so far recovered as to render it safe to return my regard more particularly upon my own case, he said to me one day,

"You would laugh at me, Campbell, were I to confess some of the bother this illness of yours has occasioned me; enough, indeed, to overthrow any conceit I ever had in my own diagnosis."

"Go on," I answered; "I promise not to laugh."

He little knew how far I should be from laughing.

"In your case," he continued, "the *pathognomic,* if you will excuse medical slang, was every now and then broken up by the intrusion of altogether foreign symptoms."

I listened with breathless attention.

"Indeed, on several occasions, when, after meditating on your case till I was worn out, I had fallen half asleep by your bedside, I came to myself with the strongest conviction that I was watching by the bedside of a woman."

"Thank Heaven!" I exclaimed, starting up, "She lives still."

I need not describe the doctor's look of amazement, almost consternation; for he thought a fresh access of fever was upon me, and I had already begun to rave. For his reassurance, however, I promised to account fully for my apparently senseless excitement; and that evening I commenced the narrative which forms the preceding part of this story. Long before I reached its close, my exultation had vanished, and, as I wrote it for him, it ended with the expressed conviction that she must be dead. Ere long, however, the hope once more revived. While, however, the narrative was in progress, I gave him a summary, which amounted to this,

I had loved a lady—loved her still. I did not know where she was, and had reason to fear that her mind had given way under the suffering of our separation. Between us there existed, as well, the bond of a distant blood relationship; so distant, that but for its probable share in the production of another relationship of a very marvellous nature, it would scarcely have been worth alluding to. This was a kind of psychological attraction, which, when justified and strengthened by the spiritual energies of love, rendered the immediate communication of certain feelings, both mental and bodily, so rapid, that almost the consciousness of the one existed for the time in the mental circumstances of the other. Nay, so complete at times was the communication, that I even doubted her testimony as to some strange correspondences in our past history on this very ground, suspecting that, my memory being open to her retrospection, she saw my story, and took it for her own. It was, therefore, easy for me to account for Dr. Ruthwell's scientific bewilderment at the symptoms I manifested.

As my health revived, my hope and longing increased. But although I loved Lady Alice with more entireness than even during the latest period of our intercourse, a certain calm endurance had supervened, which rendered the relief of fierce action no longer necessary to the continuance of a sane existence. It was as if the concentrated orb of love had diffused itself in a genial warmth through the whole orb of life, imparting fresh vitality to many roots which had remained leafless in my being. For years the field of battle was the only field that had borne the flower of delight; now nature began to live again for me.

One day, the first on which I ventured to walk into the fields alone, I was delighted with the multitude of the daisies peeping from the grass everywhere—the first attempts of the earth, become conscious of blindness, to open eyes, and see what was about and above her. Everything is wonderful after the resurrection from illness. It is a resurrection of all nature. But somehow or other I was not satisfied with the daisies. They did not seem to me so lovely as the daisies I used to see when I was a child. I thought with myself, "This is the cloud that gathers with life, the dimness that passion and suffering cast over the eyes of the mind." That moment my gaze fell upon a single, solitary, red-tipped daisy. My reasoning vanished, and my melancholy with it, slain by the red tips of the lonely beauty. This was the kind' of daisy I had loved as a child; and with the sight of it, a whole field of them rushed back into my mind—a field of my father's, where, throughout the multitude, you could not have found a white one. My father was dead; the fields had passed into other hands; but perhaps the red-tipped *gowans* were left. I must go and see. At all events, the hill that overlooked the field would still be there, and no change would have passed upon *it*. It would receive me with the same familiar look as of old, still fronting the great mountain from whose sides I had first heard the sound of that clanking horseshoe, which, whatever might be said to account for it, had certainly had a fearful connection with my joys and sorrows both. Did the ghostly rider still haunt the place? or, if he did, should I hear again that sound of coming woe? Whether or not, I defied him. I would not be turned from my desire to see the old place by any fear of a ghostly marauder, whom I should be only too glad to encounter, if there were the smallest chance of coming off with the victory.

As soon as my friend would permit me, I set out for Scotland.

CHAPTER 18

Old Friends

I MADE the journey by early stages, chiefly on the back
of a favourite black horse, which had carried me well in
several fights, and had come out of them scarred, like his
master, but sound in wind and limb. It was night when
I reached the village lying nearest to my birthplace.

When I woke in the morning, I found the whole region
filled with a white mist, hiding the mountains around.
Now and then a peak looked through, and again retired
into the cloudy folds. In the wide, straggling street,
below the window at which I had made them place my
breakfast-table, a periodical fair was being held; and I sat
looking down on the gathering crowd, trying to discover
some face known to my childhood, and still to be recog-
nized through the veil which years must have woven
across the features. When I had finished my breakfast, I

went down and wandered about among the people. Groups of elderly men were talking earnestly; and young men and maidens who had come to be *fee'd* were joking and laughing. They stared at the Sassenach gentleman, and, little thinking that he understood every word they uttered, made their remarks upon him in no very subdued tones. I approached a stall where a brown old woman was selling gingerbread and apples. She was talking to a man with long, white locks. Near them was a group of young people. One of them must have said something about me; for the old woman, who had been taking stolen glances at me, turned rather sharply towards them, and rebuked them for rudeness.

"The gentleman is no Sassenach," she said. "He understands everything you are saying."

This was spoken in Gaelic, of course. I turned and looked at her with more observance. She made me a courtesy, and said in the same language,

"Your honour will be a Campbell, I'm thinking."

"I am a Campbell," I answered and waited.

"Your honour's Christian name wouldn't be Duncan, sir?"

"It is Duncan," I answered; "but there are many Duncan Campbells."

"Only one to me, your honour; and that's yourself. But you will not remember me?"

I did not remember her. Before long, however, urged by her anxiety to associate her present with my past, she enabled me to recall in her time-worn features those of a servant in my father's house when I was a child.

"But how could you recollect me?" I said.

"I have often seen you since I left your father's, sir. But it was really, I believe, that I hear more about you than anything else, every day of my life."

"I do not understand you."

"From old Margaret, I mean."

"Dear old Margaret! Is she alive?"

"Alive and hearty, though quite bedridden. Why, sir, she must be within near sight of a hundred."

"Where does she live?"

"In the old cottage, sir. Nothing will make her leave it. The new laird wanted to turn her out; but Margaret muttered something at which he grew as white as his shirt, and he has never ventured across her threshold again."

"How do you see so much of her, though?"

"I never leave her, sir. She can't wait on herself, poor old lady. And she's like a mother to me. Bless her! But your honour will come and see her?"

"Of course I will. Tell her so when you go home."

"Will you honour me by sleeping at my house, sir?" said the old man to whom she had been talking. "My farm is just over the brow of the hill, you know."

I had by this time recognised him, and I accepted his offer at once.

"When may we look for you, sir?" he asked.

"When shall you be home?" I rejoined.

"This afternoon, sir. I have done my business already."

"Then I shall be with you in the evening, for I have nothing to keep me here."

"Will you take a seat in my gig?"

"No, thank you. I have my own horse with me. You can take him in too, I dare say?"

"With pleasure, sir."

We parted for the meantime. I rambled about the neighbourhood till it was time for an early dinner.

CHAPTER 19

Old Constancy

THE fog cleared off; and, as the hills began to throw long, lazy shadows, their only embraces across the wide valleys, I mounted and set out on the ride of a few miles which should bring me to my old acquaintance's dwelling.

I lingered on the way. All the old places demanded my notice. They seemed to say, "Here we are—waiting for you." Many a tuft of harebells drew me towards the roadside, to look at them and their children, the blue butterflies, hovering over them; and I stopped to gaze at many a wild rosebush, with a sunset of its own roses. The sun had set to me, before I had completed half the distance. But there was a long twilight, and I knew the road well.

My horse was an excellent walker, and I let him walk on, with the reins on his neck; while I, lost in a dream of the past, was singing a song of my own making, with which I often comforted my longing by giving it voice.

"The autumn winds are sighing
  Over land and sea;
The autumn woods are dying
  Over hill and lea;
And my heart is sighing, dying,
  Maiden, for thee.

The autumn clouds are flying
  Homeless over me;
The homeless birds are crying
  In the naked tree;
And my heart is flying, crying,
  Maiden, to thee.

My cries may turn to gladness,
  And my flying flee;
My sighs may lose the sadness,
  Yet sigh on in me;
All my sadness, all my gladness,
  Maiden, lost in thee."

I was roused by a heavy drop of rain upon my face. I looked up. A cool wave of wind flowed against me. Clouds had gathered; and over the peak of a hill to the left, the sky was very black. Old Constancy threw his head up, as if he wanted me to take the reins, and let him step out. I remembered that there used to be an awkward piece of road somewhere not far in front, where the path, with a bank on the left side, sloped to a deep descent on the right. If the road was as bad there as it used to be, it would be better to pass it before it grew quite dark. So

I took the reins, and away went old Constancy. We had just reached the spot, when a keen flash of lightning broke from the cloud overhead, and my horse instantly stood stock-still, as if paralysed, with his nostrils turned up towards the peak of the mountain. I sat as still as he, to give him time to recover himself. But all at once, his whole frame was convulsed, as if by an agony of terror. He gave a great plunge, and then I felt his muscles swelling and knotting under me, as he rose on his hind legs, and went backwards, with the scaur behind him. I leaned forward on his neck to bring him down, but he reared higher and higher, till he stood bolt upright, and it was time to slip off, lest he should fall upon me. I did so; but my foot alighted upon no support. He had backed to the edge of the shelving ground, and I fell, and went to the bottom. The last thing I was aware of, was the thundering fall of my horse beside me.

When I came to myself, it was dark. I felt stupid and aching all over; but I soon satisfied myself that no bones were broken. A mass of something lay near me. It was poor Constancy. I crawled to him, laid my hand on his neck, and called him by his name. But he made no answer in that gentle, joyful speech—for it was speech in old Constancy—with which he always greeted me, if only after an hour's absence. I felt for his heart. There was just a flutter there. He tried to lift his head, and gave a little kick with one of his hind legs. In doing so, he struck a bit of rock, and the clank of the iron made my flesh creep. I got hold of his leg in the dark, and felt the shoe. *It was loose.* I felt his heart again. The motion had ceased. I needed all my manhood to keep from crying like a child; for my charger was my friend. How long I lay beside him, I do not know; but, at length, I heard the sound of wheels coming along the road. I tried to shout, and, in some measure, succeeded; for a voice, which I recognised as that of my farmer-friend, answered cheerily. He was shocked to discover that his expected guest was in such evil plight. It was still dark, for the rain was falling heavily; but, with his directions, I was soon able to take my seat beside him in the gig. He had been unexpectedly detained, and was now hastening home with the hope of being yet in time to welcome me.

Next morning, after the luxurious rest of a heath-erbed, I found myself not much the worse for my adventure, but heart-sore for the loss of my horse.

CHAPTER 20

Margaret

Eᴀʀʟʏ in the forenoon, I came in sight of the cottage of Margaret. It lay unchanged, a grey, stone-fashioned hut, in the hollow of the mountain-basin. I scrambled down the soft green brae, and soon stood within the door of the cottage. There I was met and welcomed by Margaret's attendant. She led me to the bed where my old nurse lay. Her eyes were yet undimmed by years, and little change had passed upon her countenance since I parted with her on that memorable night. The moment she saw me, she broke out into a passionate lamentation such as a mother might utter over the maimed strength and disfigured beauty of her child.

"What ill has he done—my bairn—to be all night the sport of the powers of the air and the wicked of the earth? But the day will dawn for my Duncan yet, and a lovely day it will be!"

Then looking at me anxiously, she said,

"You're not much the worse for last night, my bairn. But woe's me! His grand horse, that carried him so, that I blessed the beast in my prayers!"

I knew that no one could have yet brought her the news of my accident.

"You saw me fall, then, nurse?" I said.

"That I did," she answered. "I see you oftener than you think. But there was a time when I could hardly see you at all, and I thought you were dead, my Duncan."

I stooped to kiss her. She laid the one hand that had still the power of motion upon my head, and dividing the hair, which had begun to be mixed with grey, said: "Eh! The bonny grey hairs! My Duncan's a man in spite of them!"

She searched until she found the scar of the sabre-cut.

"Just where I thought to find it!" she said. "That was a terrible day; worse for me than for you, Duncan."

"You saw me *then!*" I exclaimed.

"Little do folks know," she answered, "who think I'm lying here like a live corpse in its coffin, what liberty my soul—and that's just me—enjoys. Little do they know what I see and hear. And there's no witchcraft or evil-doing in it, my boy; but just what the Almighty made me. Janet, here, declares she heard the cry that I made, when this same cut, that's not so well healed yet, broke out in your bonny head. I saw no sword, only the bursting of the blood from the wound. But sit down, my bairn, and have something to eat after your walk. We'll have time enough for speech."

Janet had laid out the table with fare of the old homely sort, and I was a boy once more as I ate the well-known food. Every now and then I glanced towards the old face. Soon I saw that she was asleep. From her lips broke murmured sounds, so partially connected that I found it impossible to remember them; but the impression they left on my mind was something like this,

"Over the water. Yes; it is a rough sea—green and white. But over the water. There is a path for the pathless. The grass on the hill is long and cool. Never horse came there. If they once sleep in that grass, no harm can hurt them more. Over the water. Up the hill." And then she murmured the words of the psalm: "He that dwelleth in the secret place."

For an hour I sat beside her. It was evidently a sweet, natural sleep, the most wonderful sleep of all, mingled with many a broken dream-rainbow. I rose at last, and, telling Janet that I would return in the evening, went back to my quarters; for my absence from the mid-day meal would have been a disappointment to the household.

When I returned to the cottage, I found Margaret only just awaked, and greatly refreshed. I sat down beside her in the twilight, and the following conversation began,

"You said, nurse, that, some time ago, you could not see me. Did you know nothing about me all that time?"

"I took it to mean that you were ill, my dear. Shortly after you left us, the same thing happened first; but I do not think you were ill then."

"I should like to tell you all my story, dear Margaret," I said, conceiving a sudden hope of assistance from one who hovered so near the unseen that she often flitted across the borders. "But would it tire you?"

"Tire me, my child!" she said, with sudden energy. "Did I not carry you in my bosom, till I loved you more than the darling I had lost? Do I not think about you and your fortunes, till, sitting there, you are no nearer to me than when a thousand miles away? You do not know my love to you, Duncan. I have lived upon it when, I daresay, you did not care whether I was alive or dead. But that was all one to my love. When you leave me now, I shall not care much. My thoughts will only return to their old ways. I think the sight of the eyes is sometimes an intrusion between the heart and its love."

Here was philosophy, or something better, from the lips of an old Highland seeress! For me, I felt it so true, that the joy of hearing her say so turned, by a sudden metamorphosis, into freak. I pretended to rise, and said,

"Then I had better go, nurse. Good-bye."

She put out her one hand, with a smile that revealed her enjoyment of the poor humour, and said, while she held me fast,

"Nay, nay, my Duncan. A little of the scarce is sometimes dearer to us than much of the better. I shall have plenty of time to think about you when I can't see you, my boy." And her philosophy melted away into tears, that filled her two blue eyes.

"I was only joking," I said.

"Do you need to tell me that?" she rejoined, smiling. "I am not so old as to be stupid yet. But I want to hear your story. I am hungering to hear it."

"But," I whispered, "I cannot speak about it before any one else."

"I will send Janet away. Janet, I want to talk to Mr. Campbell alone."

"Very well, Margaret," answered Janet, and left the room.

"Will she listen?" I asked.

"She dares not," answered Margaret, with a smile; "she has a terrible idea of my powers."

The twilight grew deeper; the glow of the peat-fire became redder; the old woman lay still as death. And I told all the story of Lady Alice. My voice sounded to myself as I spoke, not like my own, but like its echo from the vault of some listening cave, or like the voices one hears beside as sleep is slowly creeping over the sense. Margaret did not once interrupt me. When I had finished she remained still silent, and I began to fear I had talked her asleep.

"Can you help me?" I said.

"I think I can," she answered. "Will you call Janet?" I called her.

"Make me a cup of tea, Janet. Will you have some tea with me, Duncan?"

Janet lighted a little lamp, and the tea was soon set out, with "flour-scones" and butter. But Margaret ate nothing; she only drank her tea, lifting her cup with her one trembling hand. When the remains of our repast had been removed, she said,

"Now, Janet, you can leave us; and on no account come into the room till Mr. Campbell calls you. Take the lamp with you."

Janet obeyed without a word of reply, and we were left once more alone, lighted only by the dull glow of the fire.

The night had gathered cloudy and dark without, reminding me of that night when she told me the story of the two brothers. But this time no storm disturbed the silence of the night. As soon as Janet was gone, Margaret said,

"Will you take the pillow from under my head, Duncan, my dear?"

I did so, and she lay in an almost horizontal position. With the living hand she lifted the powerless arm, and drew it across her chest, outside the bedclothes. Then she laid the other arm over it, and, looking up at me, said,

"Kiss me, my bairn; I need strength for what I am going to do for your sake."

I kissed her.

"There now!" she said, "I am ready. Good-bye. Whatever happens, do not speak to me; and let no one come near me but yourself. It will be wearisome for you, but it is for your sake, my Duncan. And don't let the fire out. Don't leave me."

I assured her I would attend to all she said. She closed her eyes, and lay still. I went to the fire, and sat down in a high-backed arm-chair, to wait the event. There was plenty of fuel in the corner. I made up the fire, and then, leaning back, with my eyes fixed on it, let my thoughts roam at will. Where was my old nurse now? What was she seeing or encountering? Would she meet our adversary? Would she be strong enough to foil him? Was she dead for the time, although some bond rendered her return from the regions of the dead inevitable? But she might never come back, and then I should have no tidings of the kind which I knew she had gone to see, and which I longed to hear!

I sat thus for a long time. I had again replenished the fire—that is all I know about the lapse of the time—when, suddenly, a kind of physical repugnance and terror seized me, and I sat upright in my chair, with every fibre of my flesh protesting against some—shall I call it presence?—in its neighbourhood. But my real self repelled the invading cold, and took courage for any contest that might be at hand. Like Macbeth, I only inhabited trembling; *I* did not tremble. I had withdrawn my gaze from the fire, and fixed it upon the little window, about two feet square, at which the dark night looked in. Why or when I had done so I knew not.

What I next relate, I relate only as what seemed to happen. I do not altogether trust myself in the matter, and think I was subjected to a delusion of some sort or other. My feelings of horror grew as I looked through or rather at the window, till, notwithstanding all my resolution and the continued assurance that nothing could make me turn my back on the cause of the terror, I was yet so far *possessed* by a feeling I could neither account for nor control, that I felt my hair rise upon my head, as if instinct with individual fear of its own—the only instance of the sort in my experience. In such a condition, the sensuous nerves are so easily operated upon, either from within or from without, that all certainty ceases.

I saw two fiery eyes looking in at the window, huge, and wide apart. Next, I saw the outline of a horse's head, in which the eyes were set; and behind, the dimmer outline of a man's form seated on the horse. The apparition faded and reappeared, just as if it retreated, and again rode up close to the window. Curiously enough, I did not even fancy that I heard any sound. Instinctively I felt for my sword, but there was no sword there. And what would it have availed me? Probably I was in more need of a soothing draught. But the moment I put my hand to the imagined sword-hilt, a dim figure swept between me and the horseman, on *my* side of the window—a tall, stately female form. She stood facing the window, in an attitude that seemed to dare the further approach of a foe. How long she remained thus, or he confronted her, I have no idea; for when *self*-consciousness returned, I found myself still gazing at the window from which both apparitions had vanished. Whether I had slept, or, from the relaxation of mental tension, had only forgotten, I could not tell; but all fear had vanished, and I proceeded at once to make up the sunken fire. Throughout the time I am certain I never heard the clanking shoe, for that I should have remembered.

The rest of the night passed without any disturbance; and when the first rays of the early morning came into the room, they awoke me from a comforting sleep in the arm-chair. I rose and approached the bed softly.

Margaret lay as still as death. But having been accustomed to similar conditions in my Alice, I believed I saw signs of returning animation, and withdrew to my seat. Nor was I mistaken; for, in a few minutes more, she murmured my name. I hastened to her.

"Call Janet," she said.

I opened the door, and called her. She came in a moment, looking at once frightened and relieved.

"Get me some tea," said Margaret once more.

After she had drunk the tea, she looked at me, and said,

"Go home now, Duncan, and come back about noon. Mind you go to bed."

She closed her eyes once more. I waited till I saw her fast in an altogether different sleep from the former, if sleep that could in any sense be called.

As I went, I looked back on the vision of the night as on one of those illusions to which the mind, busy with its own suggestions, is always liable. The night season, simply because it excludes the external, is prolific in such. The more of the marvellous any one may have experienced in the course of his history, the more sceptical ought he to become, for he is the more exposed to delusion. None have made more blunders in the course of their revelations than genuine seers. Was it any wonder that, as I sat at midnight beside the woman of a hundred years, who had voluntarily died for a time that she might discover what most of all things it concerned me to know, the ancient tale, on which, to her mind, my whole history turned, and which she had herself told me in this very cottage, should take visible shape to my excited brain and watching eyes?

I have one thing more to tell, which strengthens still further this view of the matter. As I walked home, before I had gone many hundred yards from the cottage, I suddenly came upon my own old Constancy. He was limping about, picking the best grass he could find from among the roots of the heather and cranberry bushes. He gave a start when I came upon him, and then a jubilant neigh.

But he could not be so glad as I was. When I had taken sufficient pains to let him know this fact, I walked on, and he followed me like a dog, with his head at my heel; but as he limped much, I turned to examine him; and found one cause of his lameness to be, that the loose shoe, which was a hind one, was broken at the toe; and that one half, held only at the toe, had turned round and was sticking right out, striking his forefoot every time he moved. I soon remedied this, and he walked much better.

But the phenomena of the night, and the share my old horse might have borne in them, were not the subjects, as may well be supposed, that occupied my mind most, on my walk to the farm. Was it possible that Margaret might have found out something about *her?* That was the one question.

After removing the anxiety of my hostess, and partaking of their Highland breakfast, a ceremony not to be completed without a glass of peaty whisky, I wandered to my ancient haunt on the hill. Thence I could look down on my old home, where it lay unchanged, though not one human form, which had made it home to me, moved about its precincts. I went no nearer. I no more felt that that was home than one feels that the form in the coffin is the departed dead. I sat down in my old study-chamber among the rocks, and thought that if I could but find Alice she would be my home—of the past as well as of the future—for in her mind my necromantic words would recall the departed, and we should love them together.

Towards noon I was again at the cottage.

Margaret was sitting up in bed, waiting for me. She looked weary, but cheerful; and a clean white *mutch* gave her a certain *company*-air. Janet left the room directly, and Margaret motioned me to a chair by her side. I sat down. She took my hand, and said,

"Duncan, my boy, I fear I can give you but little help; but I will tell you all I know. If I were to try to put into words the things I had to encounter before I could come near her, you would not understand what I meant. Nor do I understand the things myself. They seem quite plain to me at the time, but very cloudy when I come back. But I did succeed in getting one glimpse of her. She was fast asleep. She seemed to have suffered much, for her face was very thin, and as patient as it was pale."

"But where was she?"

"I must leave you to find out that, if you can, from my description. But, alas! it is only the places immediately about the persons that I can see. Where they are, or how far I have gone to get there, I cannot tell."

She then gave me a rather minute description of the chamber in which the lady was lying. Though most of the particulars were unknown to me, the conviction, or hope at least, gradually dawned upon me, that I knew the room. Once or twice I had peeped into the sanctuary of Lady Alice's chamber, when I knew she was not there; and some points in the description Margaret gave set my heart in a tremor with the bare suggestion that she might now be at Hilton Hall.

"Tell me, Margaret," I said, almost panting for utterance, "was there a mirror over the fireplace, with a broad gilt frame, carved into huge representations of crabs and lobsters, and all crawling sea-creatures with shells on them—very ugly, and very strange?"

She would have interrupted me before, but I would not be stopped.

"I must tell you, my dear Duncan," she answered, "that in none of these trances, or whatever you please to call them, did I ever see a mirror. It has struck me before as a curious thing, that a mirror is then an absolute blank to me—I see nothing on which I could put a name. It does not even seem a vacant space to me. A mirror must have nothing in common with the state I am then in, for I feel a kind of repulsion from it; and indeed it would be rather an awful thing to look at, for of course I should see no reflection of myself in it."

(Here I beg once more to remind the reader, that Margaret spoke in Gaelic, and that my translation into ordinary English does not in the least represent the extreme simplicity of the forms of her speculations, any more than of the language which conveyed them.)

"But," she continued, "I have a vague recollection of seeing some broad, big, gilded thing with figures on it. It might be something else, though, altogether."

"I will go in hope," I answered, rising at once.

"Not already, Duncan?"

"Why should I stay longer?"

"Stay over to-night."

"What is the use? I cannot."

"For my sake, Duncan!"

"Yes, dear Margaret; for your sake. Yes, surely."

"Thank you," she answered. "I will not keep you longer now. But if I send Janet to you, come at once.

And, Duncan, wear this for my sake."

She put into my hand an ancient gold cross, much worn. To my amazement I recognised the counterpart of one Lady Alice had always worn. I pressed it to my heart.

"I am a Catholic; you are a Protestant, Duncan; but never mind: that's the same sign to both of us. You won't part with it. It has been in *our* family for many long years."

"Not while I live," I answered, and went out, half wild with hope, into the keen mountain air. How deliciously it breathed upon me!

I passed the afternoon in attempting to form some plan of action at Hilton Hall, whither I intended to proceed as soon as Margaret set me at liberty. That liberty came sooner than I expected; and yet I did not go at once. Janet came for me towards sundown. I thought she looked troubled. I rose at once and followed her, but asked no questions. As I entered the cottage, the sun was casting the shadow of the edge of the hollow in which the cottage stood just at my feet; that is, the sun was more than half set to one who stood at the cottage door. I entered.

Margaret sat, propped with pillows. I saw some change had passed upon her. She held out out her hand to me. I took it. She smiled feebly, closed her eyes, and went with the sun, down the hill of night. But down the hill of night is up the hill of morning in other lands, and no doubt Margaret soon found that she was more at home there than here.

I sat holding the dead hand, as if therein lay some communion still with the departed. Perhaps she who saw more than others while yet alive, could see when dead that I held her cold hand in my warm grasp. Had I not good cause to love her? She had exhausted the last remnants of her life in that effort to find for me my lost Alice. Whether she had succeeded I had yet to discover. Perhaps she knew now.

I hastened the funeral a little, that I might follow my quest. I had her grave dug amidst her own people and mine; for they lay side by side. The whole neighbourhood for twenty miles round followed Margaret to the grave. Such was her character and reputation, that the belief in her supernatural powers had only heightened the notion of the venerableness.

When I had seen the last sod placed on her grave, I turned and went, with a desolate but hopeful heart. I had a kind of feeling that her death had sealed the truth of her last vision. I mounted old Constancy at the churchyard gate, and set out for Hilton Hall.

CHAPTER 21

Hilton

IT was a dark, drizzling night when I arrived at the little village of Hilton, within a mile of the Hall. I knew a respectable second-rate inn on the side next the Hall, to which the gardener and other servants had been in the habit of repairing of an evening; and I thought I might there stumble upon some information, especially as the old-fashioned place had a large kitchen in which all sorts of guests met. When I reflected on the utter change which time, weather, and a great scar must have made upon me, I feared no recognition. But what was my surprise when, by one of those coincidences which have so often happened to me, I found in the ostler one of my own troop at Waterloo! His countenance and salute convinced me that he recognised me. I said to him,

"I know you perfectly, Wood; but you must not know me. I will go with you to the stable."

He led the way instantly.

"Wood," I said, when we had reached the shelter of the stable, "I don't want to be known here, for reasons which I will explain to you another time."

"Very well, sir. You may depend on me, sir."

"I know I may, and I shall. Do you know anybody about the Hall?"

"Yes, sir. The gardener comes here sometimes, sir. I believe he's in the house now. Shall I ask him to step this way, sir?"

"No. All I want is to learn who is at the Hall now. Will you get him talking? I shall be by, having something to drink."

"Yes, sir. As soon as I have rubbed down the old horse, sir—bless him!"

"You'll find me there."

I went in, and, with my condition for an excuse, ordered something hot by the kitchen fire. Several country people were sitting about it. They made room for me, and I took my place at a table on one side. I soon discovered the gardener, although Time had done what he could to disguise him. Wood came in presently, and, loitering about, began to talk to him.

"What's the last news at the Hall, William?" he said.

"News!" answered the old man, somewhat querulously. "There's never nothing but news up there, and very new-fangled news, too. What do you think, now, John? They do talk of turning all them greenhouses into hothouses; for, to be sure, there's nothing the new missus cares about but just the finest grapes in the country; and the flowers, purty creatures, may go to the devil for her. There's a lady for ye!"

"But you'll be glad to have her home, and see what she's like, won't you? It's rather dull up there now, isn't it?"

"I don't know what you call dull," replied the old man, as if half offended at the suggestion. "I don't believe a soul missed his lordship when he died; and there's always Mrs. Blakesley and me, as is the best friends in the world, besides the three maids and the stableman, who helps me in the garden, now there's no horses. And then there's Jacob and—"

"But you don't mean," said Wood, interrupting him, "that there's *none* o' the family at home now?"

"No. Who should there be? Leastways, only the poor lady. And she hardly counts now—bless her sweet face!"

"Do you ever see her?" interposed one of the bysitters.

"Sometimes."

"Is she quite crazy?"

"Al-to-gether; but that quiet *and* gentle, you would think she was an angel instead of a mad woman. But not a notion has she in *her* head, no more than the babe unborn."

It was a dreadful shock to me. Was this to be the end of all? Were it not better she had died? For me, life was worthless now. And there were no wars, with the chance of losing it honestly.

I rose, and went to my own room. As I sat in dull misery by the fire, it struck me that it might not have been Lady Alice after all that the old man spoke about. That moment a tap came to my door, and Wood entered. After a few words, I asked him who was the lady the gardener had said was crazy.

"Lady Alice," he answered, and added: "A love story, that came to a bad end up at the Hall years ago. A tutor was in it, they say. But I don't know the rights of it."

When he left me, I sat in a cold stupor, in which the thoughts—if thoughts they could be called—came and went of themselves. Overcome by the appearances of things—as what man the strongest may not sometimes be?—I felt as if I had lost her utterly, as if there was no Lady Alice anywhere, and as if, to add to the vacant horror of the world without her, a shadow of her, a goblin *simulacrum,* soulless, unreal, yet awfully like her, went wandering about the place which had once been glorified by her presence—as to the eyes of seers the phantoms of events which have happened years before are still visible, clinging to the room in which they have indeed *taken place.* But, in a little while, something warm began to throb and flow in my being; and I thought that if she were dead, I should love her still; that now she was not worse than dead; it was only that her soul was out of sight. Who could tell but it might be wandering in worlds of too noble shapes and too high a speech, to permit of representation in the language of the world in which her bodily presentation remained, and therefore her speech and behaviour seemed to men to be mad? Nay, was it not in some sense better for me that it should be so? To see once the pictured likeness of her of whom I had no such memorial, would I not give years of my poverty-stricken life? And here was such a statue of her, as that of his wife which the widowed king was bending before, when he said,

"What fine chisel
Could ever yet cut breath?"

This statue I might see, "looking like an angel," as the
gardener had said. And, while the bond of visibility remained, must not the soul be, somehow, nearer to the
earth, than if the form lay decaying beneath it? Was there
not some possibility that the love for whose sake the
reason had departed, might be able to recall that reason
once more to the windows of sense—make it look forth
at those eyes, and lie listening in the recesses of those
ears? In her somnambulic sleeps, the present body was
the sign that the soul was within reach: so it might be still.

Mrs. Blakesley was still at the lodge, then: I would call
upon her to-morrow. I went to bed, and dreamed all
night that Alice was sitting somewhere in a land "full of
dark mountains," and that I was wandering about in the
darkness, alternately calling and listening; sometimes
fancying I heard a faint reply, which might be her voice
or an echo of my own; but never finding her. I woke in
an outburst of despairing tears, and my despair was not
comforted by my waking.

CHAPTER 22

The Sleeper

IT was a lovely morning in autumn. I walked to the Hall. I entered at the same gate by which I had entered first, so many years before. But it was not Mrs. Blakesley that opened it. I inquired after her, and the woman told me that she lived at the Hall now, and took care of Lady Alice. So far, this was hopeful news.

I went up the same avenue, through the same wide grassy places, saw the same statue from whose base had arisen the lovely form which soon became a part of my existence. Then everything looked rich, because I had come from a poor, grand country. In all my wanderings I had seen nothing so rich; yet now it seemed poverty-stricken. That it was autumn could not account for this; for I had always found that the sadness of autumn vivified the poetic sense, and that the colours of decay had a pathetic glory more beautiful than the glory of the most gorgeous summer with all its flowers. It was winter within me—that was the reason; and I could feel no autumn around me, because I saw no spring beyond me. It had fared with my mind as with the garden in the *Sensitive Plant,* when the lady was dead. I was amazed and troubled at the stolidity with which I walked up to the door, and, having rung the bell, waited. No sweet memories of the past arose in my mind; not one of the well-known objects around looked at me as claiming a recognition. Yet, when the door was opened, my heart beat so violently at the thought that I might see her, that I could hardly stammer out my inquiry after Mrs. Blakesley.

I was shown to a room. None of the sensations I had had on first crossing the threshold were revived. I remembered them all; I felt none of them. Mrs. Blakesley came. She did not recognise me. I told her who I was. She stared at me for a moment, seemed to see the same face she had known still glimmering through all the changes that had crowded upon it, held out both her hands, and burst into tears.

"Mr. Campbell," she said, "you *are* changed! But not like her. She's the same to look at; but, oh dear!"

We were both silent for some time. At length she resumed,

"Come to my room; I have been mistress here for some time now."

I followed her to the room Mrs. Wilson used to occupy. She put wine on the table. I told her my story. My labours, and my wounds, and my illness, slightly touched as I trust they were in the course of the tale, yet moved all her womanly sympathies.

"What can I do for you, Mr. Campbell?" she said.

"Let me see her," I replied.

She hesitated for a moment.

"I dare not, sir. I don't know what it might do to her. It might send her raving; and she is so quiet."

"Has she ever raved?"

"Not often since the first week or two. Now and then occasionally, for an hour or so, she would be wild, wanting to get out. But she gave that over altogether; and she has had her liberty now for a long time. But, Heaven bless her! at the worst she was always a lady."

"And am I to go away without even seeing her?"

"I am very sorry for you, Mr. Campbell."

I felt hurt—foolishly, I confess—and rose. She put her hand on my arm.

"I'll tell you what I'll do, sir. She always falls asleep in the afternoon; you may see her asleep, if you like."

"Thank you; thank you," I answered. "That will be much better. When shall I come?"

"About three o'clock."

I went wandering about the woods, and at three I was again in the housekeeper's room. She came to me presently, looking rather troubled.

"It is very odd," she began, the moment she entered, "but for the first time, I think, for years, she's not for her afternoon sleep."

"Does she sleep at night?" I asked.

"Like a bairn. But she sleeps a great deal; and the doctor says that's what keeps her so quiet. She would go raving again, he says, if the sleep did not soothe her poor brain."

"Could you not let me see her when she is asleep to-night?"

Again she hesitated, but presently replied,

"I will, sir; but I trust to you never to mention it."

"Of course I will not."

"Come at ten o'clock, then. You will find the outer door on this side open. Go straight to my room."

With renewed thanks I left her and, once again betaking myself to the woods, wandered about till night, notwithstanding signs of an approaching storm. I thus kept within the boundaries of the demesne, and had no occasion to request readmittance at any of the gates.

As ten struck on the tower clock, I entered Mrs. Blakesley's room. She was not there. I sat down. In a few minutes she came.

"She is fast asleep," she said. "Come this way."

I followed, trembling. She led me to the same room Lady Alice used to occupy. The door was a little open. She pushed it gently, and I followed her in. The curtains towards the door were drawn. Mrs. Blakesley took me round to the other side. There lay the lovely head, so phantom-like for years, coming only in my dreams; filling now, with a real presence, the eyes that had longed for it, as if in them dwelt an appetite of sight. It calmed my heart at once, which had been almost choking me with the violence of its palpitation. "That is not the face of insanity," I said to myself. "It is clear as the morning light." As I stood gazing, I made no comparisons between the past and the present, although I was aware of

some difference—of some measure of the unknown
fronting me; I was filled with the delight of beholding the
face I loved—full, as it seemed to me, of mind and wom-
anhood; sleeping—nothing more. I murmured a fervent
"Thank God!" and was turning away with a feeling of
satisfaction for all the future, and a strange great hope
beginning to throb in my heart, when, after a little restless motion of her head on the pillow, her patient lips
began to tremble. My soul rushed into my ears.

"Mr. Campbell," she murmured, "I cannot spell; what
am I to do to learn?"

The unexpected voice, naming my name, sounded in
my ears like a voice from the far-off regions where sighing is over. Then a smile gleamed up from the depths
unseen, and broke and melted away all over her face. But
her nurse had heard her speak, and now approached in
alarm. She laid hold of my arm, and drew me towards the
door. I yielded at once, but heard a moan from the bed
as I went. I looked back—the curtains hid her from my
view. Outside the door, Mrs. Blakesley stood listening
for a moment, and then led the way downstairs.

"You made her restless. You see, sir, she never was
like other people, poor dear!"

"Her face is not like one insane," I rejoined.

"I often think she looks more like herself when she's
asleep," answered she. "And then I have often seen her
smile. She never smiles when she's awake. But, gracious
me, Mr. Campbell! what *shall* I do?"

This exclamation was caused by my suddenly falling
back in my chair and closing my eyes. I had almost
fainted. I had eaten nothing since breakfast; and had

been wandering about in a state of excitement all day. I greedily swallowed the glass of wine she brought me, and then first became aware that the storm which I had seen gathering while I was in the woods had now broken loose. "What a night in the old hall!" thought I. The wind was dashing itself like a thousand eagles against the house, and the rain was trampling the roofs and the court like troops of galloping steeds. I rose to go.

But Mrs. Blakesley interfered.

"You don't leave this house to-night, Mr. Campbell," she said. "I won't have your death laid at my door."

I laughed.

"Dear Mrs. Blakesley—" I said, seeing her determined.

"I won't hear a word," she interrupted. "I wouldn't let a horse out in such a tempest. No, no; you shall just sleep in your old quarters, across the passage there."

I did not care for any storm. It hardly even interested me. That beautiful face filled my whole being. But I yielded to Mrs. Blakesley, and not unwillingly.

CHAPTER 23

My Old Room

ONCE more I was left alone in that room of dark oak, looking out on the little ivy-mantled court, of which I was now reminded by the howling of the storm within its high walls. Mrs. Blakesley had extemporised a bed for me on the old sofa; and the fire was already blazing away splendidly. I sat down beside it, and the sombre-hued Past rolled back upon me.

After I had floated, as it were, upon the waves of memory for some time, I suddenly glanced behind me and around the room, and a new and strange experience dawned upon me. Time became to my consciousness what some metaphysicians say it is in itself—only a *form* of human thought. For the Past had returned and had become the Present. I could not be sure that the Past had passed, that I had not been dreaming through the whole series of years and adventures, upon which I was able to look back. For here was the room, all as before; and here was I, the same man, with the same love glowing in my heart. I went on thinking. The storm went on howling. The logs went on cheerily burning. I rose and walked about the room, looking at everything as I had looked at it on the night of my first arrival. I said to myself, "How strange that I should feel as if all this had happened to me before!" And then I said, "Perhaps it *has* happened to me before." Again I said, "And when it did happen before, I felt as if it had happened before that; and perhaps it has been happening to me at intervals for ages." I opened the door of the closet, and looked at the door behind it, which led into the hall of the old house. It was bolted. But the bolt slipped back at my touch; twelve years were nothing in the history of its rust; or was it only yesterday I had forced the iron free from the adhesion of the rust-welded surfaces? I stood for a moment hesitating whether to open the door, and have one peep into the wide hall, full of intent echoes, listening breathless for one air of sound, that they might catch it up jubilant and dash it into the ears of Silence—their ancient enemy —their Death. But I drew back, leaving the door unopened; and, sitting down again by my fire, sank into a kind of unconscious weariness. Perhaps I slept—I do not know; but as I became once more aware of myself, I awoke, as it were, in the midst of an old long-buried night. I was sitting in my own room, waiting for Lady Alice. And, as I sat waiting, and wishing she would come, by slow degrees my wishes intensified themselves, till I found myself, with all my gathered might, willing that she should come. The minutes passed, but the will remained.

How shall I tell what followed? The door of the closet opened—slowly, gently—and in walked Lady Alice, pale as death, her eyes closed, her whole person asleep. With a gliding motion as in a dream, where the volition that produces motion is unfelt, she seemed to me to dream herself across the floor to my couch, on which she laid herself down as gracefully, as simply, as in the old beautiful time. Her appearance did not startle me, for my whole condition was in harmony with the phenomenon. I rose noiselessly, covered her lightly from head to foot, and sat down, as of old to watch. How beautiful she was! I thought she had grown taller; but, perhaps, it was only that she had gained in form without losing anything in grace. Her face was, as it had always been, colourless; but neither it nor her figure showed any signs of suffering. The holy sleep had fed her physical as well as shielded her mental nature. But what would the waking be? Not all the power of the revived past could shut out the anticipation of the dreadful difference to be disclosed, the moment she should open those sleeping eyes. To what a frightfully farther distance was that soul now removed, whose return I had been wont to watch, as from the depths of the unknown world! That was strange; this was terrible. Instead of the dawn of rosy intelligence I had now to look for the fading of the loveliness as she woke, till her face withered into the bewildered and indigent expression of the insane.

She was waking. My love with the unknown face was at hand. The reviving flush came, grew, deepened. She opened her eyes. God be praised! They were lovelier than ever. And the smile that broke over her face was the very sunlight of the soul.

"Come again, you see!" she said gently, as she stretched her beautiful arms towards me.

I could not speak. I could only submit to her embrace, and hold myself with all my might, lest I should burst into helpless weeping. But a sob or two broke their prison, and she felt the emotion she had not seen. Relaxing her hold, she pushed me gently from her, and looked at me with concern that grew as she looked.

"You are dreadfully changed, my Duncan! What is the matter? Has Lord Hilton been rude to you? You look so much older, somehow. What can it be?"

I understood at once how it was. The whole of those dreary twelve years was gone. The thread of her consciousness had been cut, those years dropped out, and the ends reunited. She thought this was one of her old visits to me, when, as now, she had walked in her sleep. I answered,

"I will tell you all another time. I don't want to waste the moments with you, my Alice, in speaking about it. Lord Hilton *has* behaved very badly to me; but never mind."

She half rose in anger; and her eyes looked insane for the first time.

"How dares he?" she said, and then checked herself with a sigh at her own helplessness.

"But it will all come right, Alice," I went on in terror lest I should disturb her present conception of her circumstances. I felt as if the very face I wore, with the changes of those twelve forgotten years, which had passed over her like the breath of a spring wind, were a mask of which I had to be ashamed before her. Her consciousness was my involuntary standard of fact. Hope of my life as she was, there was thus mingled with my delight in her presence a restless fear that made me wish fervently that she would go. I wanted time to quiet my thoughts and resolve how I should behave to her.

"Alice," I said, "it is nearly morning. You were late to-night. Don't you think you had better go—for fear, you know?"

"Ah!" she said, with a smile, in which there was no doubt of fear, "you are tired of me already! But I will go at once—to dream about you."

She rose.

"Go, my darling," I said; "and mind you get some right sleep. Shall I go with you?"

Much to my relief, she answered,

"No, no; please not. I can go alone as usual. When a ghost meets me, I just walk through him, and then he's nowhere; and I laugh."

One kiss, one backward lingering look, and the door closed behind her. I heard the echo of the great hall. I was alone. But what a loneliness—a loneliness crowded with presence! I paced up and down the room, threw myself on the couch she had left, started up, and paced again. It was long before I could think. But the conviction grew upon me that she would be mine yet. Mine yet? Mine she *was,* beyond all the power of madness or demons; and mine I trusted she would be beyond the dispute of the world. About me, at least, she was not insane.

But what should I do? The only chance of her recovery
lay in seeing me still; but I could resolve on nothing till
I knew whether Mrs. Blakesley had discovered her absence from her room; because, if I drew her, and she
were watched and prevented from coming, it would kill
her, or worse. I must take to-morrow to think.

Yet at the moment, by a sudden impulse, I opened the
window gently, stepped into the little grassy court, where
the last of the storm was still moaning, and withdrew the
bolts of a door which led into an alley of trees running
along one side of the kitchen garden. I felt like a housebreaker; but I said, "It is *her* right." I pushed the bolts
forward again, so as just to touch the sockets and look as
if they went in, and then retreated into my own room,
where I paced about till the household was astir.

CHAPTER 24

Prison-Breaking

ᘑᘐ

Iᴛ was with considerable anxiety that I repaired to Mrs. Blakesley's room. There I found the old lady at the breakfast-table, so thoroughly composed, that I was at once reassured as to her ignorance of what had occurred while she slept. But she seemed uneasy till I should take my departure, which I attributed to the fear that I might happen to meet Lady Alice.

Arrived at my inn, I kept my room, my dim-seen plans rendering it desirable that I should attract as little attention in the neighbourhood as might be. I had now to concentrate these plans, and make them definite to myself. It was clear that there was no chance of spending another night at Hilton Hall by invitation: would it be honourable to go there without one, as I, knowing all the *outs and ins* of the place, could, if I pleased? I went over

the whole question of Alice's position in that house, and
of the crime committed against her. I saw that, if I could
win my wife by restoring to her the exercise of reason,
that very success would justify the right I already possessed in her. And could she not demand of me to climb
over any walls, or break open whatsoever doors, to free
her from her prison—from the darkness of a clouded
brain? Let them say what they would of the meanness
and wickedness of gaining such access to, and using such
power over, the insane—she was mine, and as safe with
me as with her mother. There is a love that tears and
destroys; and there is a love that enfolds and saves. I
hated mesmerism and its vulgar impertinences; but here
was a power I possessed, as far as I knew, only over one,
and that one allied to me by a reciprocal influence, as
well as long-tried affection. Did not love give me the
right to employ this power?

My cognition concluded in the resolve to use the
means in my hands for the rescue of Lady Alice. Midnight found me in the alley of the kitchen garden. The
door of the little court opened easily. Nor had I withdrawn its bolts without knowing that I could manage to
open the window of my old room from the outside. I
stood in the dark, a stranger and housebreaker, where so
often I had sat waiting the visits of my angel. I secured
the door of the room, struck a light, lighted a remnant
of taper which I found on the table, threw myself on the
couch, and said to my Alice, "Come."

And she came. I rose. She laid herself down. I pulled
off my coat—it was all I could find—and laid it over her.
The night was chilly. She revived with the same sweet

smile, but, giving a little shiver, said,

"Why have you no fire, Duncan? I must give orders about it. That's some trick of old Clankshoe."

"Dear Alice, do not breath a word about me to any one. I have quarrelled with Lord Hilton. He has turned me away, and I have no business to be in the house."

"Oh!" she replied, with a kind of faint recollecting hesitation. "That must be why you never come to the haunted chamber now. I go there every night, as soon as the sun is down."

"Yes, that is it, Alice."

"Ah! that must be what makes the day so strange to me too."

She looked very bewildered for a moment, and then resumed,

"Do you know, Duncan, I feel very strange all day—as if I was walking about in a dull dream that would never come to an end? But it is very different at night—is it not, dear?"

She had not yet discovered any distinction between my presence to her dreams and my presence to her waking sight. I hardly knew what reply to make; but she went on,

"They won't let me come to you now, I suppose. I shall forget my Euclid and everything. I feel as if I had forgotten it all already. But you won't be vexed with your poor Alice, will you? She's only a beggar-girl, you know."

I could answer only by a caress.

"I had a strange dream the other night. I thought I was sitting on a stone in the dark. And I heard your voice calling me. And it went all round about me, and came nearer, and went farther off, but I could not move to go to you. I tried to answer you, but I could only make a queer sound, not like my own voice at all."

"I dreamed it too, Alice."

"The same dream?"

"Yes, the very same."

"I am so glad. But I didn't like the dream. Duncan, my head feels so strange sometimes. And I am so sleepy. Duncan, dearest—*am* I dreaming now? Oh! tell me that I am awake and that I hold you; for to-morrow, when I wake, I shall fancy that I have lost you. They've spoiled my poor brain, somehow. I am all right, I know, but I cannot get at it. The red is withered, somehow."

"You are wide awake, my Alice. I know all about it. I will help you to understand it all, only you must do exactly as I tell you."

"Yes, yes."

"Then go to bed now, and sleep as much as you can; else I will not let you come to me at night."

"That would be too cruel, when it is all I have."

"Then go, dearest, and sleep."

"I will."

She rose and went. I, too, went, making all close behind me. The moon was going down. Her light looked to me strange, and almost malignant. I feared that when she came to the full she would hurt my darling's brain, and I longed to climb the sky, and cut her in pieces. Was I too going mad? I needed rest, that was all.

Next morning, I called again upon Mrs. Blakesley, to inquire after Lady Alice, anxious to know how yesterday had passed.

"Just the same," answered the old lady. "You need not

look for any change. Yesterday I did see her smile once, though."

And was that nothing?

In her case there was a reversal of the usual facts of nature (I say *facts,* not *laws*): the dreams of most people are more or less insane; those of Lady Alice were sound; thus, with her, restoring the balance of sane life. That smile was the sign of the dream-life beginning to leaven the waking and false life.

"Have you heard of young Lord Hilton's marriage?" asked Mrs. Blakesley.

"I have only heard some rumours about it," I answered. "Who is the new countess?"

"The daughter of a rich merchant somewhere. They say she isn't the best of tempers. They're coming here in about a month. I am just terrified to think how it may fare with my lamb now. They won't let her go wandering about wherever she pleases, I doubt. And if they shut her up, she will die."

I vowed inwardly that she should be free, if I carried her off, madness and all.

CHAPTER 25

New Entrenchments

But this way of breaking into the house every night did not afford me the facility I wished. For I wanted to see Lady Alice during the day, or at least in the evening before she went to sleep; as otherwise I could not thoroughly judge of her condition. So I got Wood to pack up a small stock of provisions for me in his haversack, which I took with me; and when I entered the house that night, I bolted the door of the court behind me, and made all fast.

I waited till the usual time for her appearance had passed; and, always apprehensive now, as was very natural, I had begun to grow uneasy, when I heard her voice, as I had heard it once before, singing. Fearful of disturbing her, I listened for a moment. Whether the song was her own or not, I cannot be certain. When I questioned her afterwards, she knew nothing about it. It was this:

> "Days of old,
> Ye are not dead, though gone from me;
> Ye are not cold,
> But like the summer-birds gone o'er the sea.
> The sun brings back the swallows fast,
> O'er the sea:
> When thou comest at the last,
> The days of old come back to me."

She ceased singing. Still she did not enter. I went into the closet, and found that the door was bolted. When I opened it, she entered, as usual; and, when she came to herself, seemed still better than before.

"Duncan," she said, "I don't know how it is, but I believe I must have forgotten everything I ever knew. I feel as if I had. I don't think I can even read. Will you teach me my letters?"

She had a book in her hand. I hailed this as another sign that her waking and sleeping thoughts bordered on each other; for she must have taken the book during her somnambulic condition. I did as she desired. She seemed to know nothing till I told her. But the moment I told her anything, she knew it perfectly. Before she left me that night she was reading tolerably, with many pauses of laughter that she should ever have forgotten how. The moment she shared the light of my mind, all was plain; where that had not shone, all was dark. The fact was, she was living still in the shadow of that shock which her nervous constitution had received from our discovery and my ejection.

As she was leaving me, I said,

"Shall you be in the haunted room at sunset to-morrow, Alice?"

"Of course I shall," she answered.

"You will find me there then," I rejoined, "that is, if you think there is no danger of being seen."

"Not the least," she answered. "No one follows me there; not even Mrs. Blakesley, good soul! They are all afraid, as usual."

"And you won't be frightened to see me there?"

"Frightened? No. Why? Oh! *you* think me queer too, do you?"

She looked vexed, but tried to smile.

"I? I would trust you with my life," I said. "That's not much, though—with my soul, whatever that means, Alice."

"Then don't talk nonsense," she rejoined coaxingly, "about my being frightened to see you."

When she had gone, I followed into the old hall, taking my sack with me; for, after having found the door in the closet bolted, I was determined not to spend one night more in my old quarters, and never to allow Lady Alice to go there again, if I could prevent her. And I had good hopes that, if we met in the day, the same consequences would follow as had followed long ago—namely, that she would sleep at night.

It was just such a night as that on which I had first peeped into the hall. The moon shone through one of the high windows, scarcely more dim than before, and showed all the dreariness of the place. I went up the great old staircase, hoping I trod in the very footsteps of Lady Alice, and reached the old gallery in which I had found her on that night when our strangely knit intimacy began. My object was to choose one of the deserted rooms in which I might establish myself without chance of discovery. I had not turned many corners, or gone through many passages, before I found one exactly to my mind. I will not trouble my reader with a description of its odd position and shape. All I wanted was concealment, and that it provided plentifully. I lay down on the floor, and was soon fast asleep.

Next morning, having breakfasted from the contents of my bag, I proceeded to make myself thoroughly acquainted with the bearings, etc., of this portion of the house. Before evening, I knew it all thoroughly.

But I found it very difficult to wait for the evening. By the windows of one of the rooms looking westward, I sat watching the down-going of the sun. When he set, my moon would rise. As he touched the horizon, I went the old, well-known way to the haunted chamber. What a night had passed for me since I left Alice in that charmed room! I had a vague feeling, however, notwithstanding the misfortune that had befallen us there, that the old phantoms that haunted it were friendly to Alice and me. But I waited her arrival in fear. Would she come? Would she be as in the night? Or should I find her but half awake to life, and perhaps asleep to me?

One moment longer, and a light hand was laid on the door. It opened gently, and Alice, entering, flitted across the room straight to my arms. How beautiful she was! her old-fashioned dress bringing her into harmony with the room and its old consecrated twilight! For this room looked eastward, and there was only twilight here. She brought me some water, at my request; and then we read, and laughed over our reading. Every moment she not only knew something fresh, but knew that she had known it before. The dust of the years had to be swept away; but it was only dust, and flew at a breath. The light soon failed us in that dusky chamber; and we sat and whispered, till only when we kissed could we see each other's eyes. At length Lady Alice said,

"They are looking for me; I had better go. Shall I come at night?"

"No," I answered. "Sleep, and do not move."

"Very well, I will."

She went, and I returned to my den. There I lay and thought. Had she ever been insane at all? I doubted it. A kind of mental sleep or stupor had come upon her—nothing more. True it might be allied to madness; but is there a strong emotion that man or woman experiences that is not *allied* to madness? Still her mind was not clear enough to reflect the past. But if she never recalled that entirely, not the less were her love and tenderness—all womanliness—entire in her.

Next evening we met again, and the next, and many evenings. Every time I was more convinced than before that she was thoroughly sane in every practical sense, and that she would recall everything as soon as I reminded her. But this I forbore to do, fearing a reaction.

Meantime, after a marvellous fashion, I was living over again the old lovely time that had gone by twelve years ago; living it over again, partly in virtue of the oblivion that had invaded the companion and source of the blessedness of the time. She had never ceased to live it; but had renewed it in dreams, unknown as such, from which she awoke to forgetfulness and quiet, while I awoke from my troubled fancies to tears and battles.

It was strange, indeed, to live the past over again thus.

CHAPTER 26

Escape

It was time, however, to lay some plan, and make some preparations, for our departure. The first thing to be secured was a convenient exit from the house. I searched in all directions, but could discover none better than that by which I had entered. Leaving the house one evening, as soon as Lady Alice had retired, I communicated my situation to Wood, who entered with all his heart into my projects. Most fortunately, through all her so-called madness, Lady Alice had retained and cherished the feeling that there was something sacred about the diamond ring and the little money which had been intended for our flight before; and she had kept them carefully concealed, where she could find them in a moment. I had sent the ring to a friend in London, to sell it for me; and it produced more than I expected. I had then commissioned Wood to go to the county town and buy a light gig for me; and in this he had been very fortunate. My dear old Constancy had the accomplishment, not at all common to chargers, of going admirably in harness; and I had from the first enjoined upon Wood to get him into as good condition as possible. I now fixed a certain hour at which Wood was to be at a certain spot on one of the roads skirting the park, where I had found a crazy door in the plank-fence—with Constancy in the dogcart, and plenty of wraps for Alice.

"And for heaven's sake, Wood," I concluded, "look to his shoes."

It may seem strange that I should have been able to go and come thus without detection; but it must be remembered that I had made myself more familiar with the place than any of its inhabitants, and that there were only a very few domestics in the establishment. The gardener and stableman slept in the house, for its protection; but I knew their windows perfectly, and most of their movements. I could watch them all day long, if I liked, from some loophole or other of my quarter; where, indeed, I sometimes found that the only occupation I could think of.

The next evening I said, "Alice, I must leave the house; will you go with me?"

"Of course I will, Duncan. When?"

"The night after to-morrow, as soon as every one is in bed and the house quiet. If you have anything you value very much, take it; but the lighter we go the better."

"I have nothing, Duncan. I will take a little bag—that will do for me."

"But dress as warmly as you can. It will be cold."

"Oh, yes; I won't forget that. Good-night."

She took it as quietly as going to church.

I had not seen Mrs. Blakesley since she had told me that the young earl and countess were expected in about a month; else I might have learned one fact which it was very important I should have known, namely, that their arrival had been hastened by eight or ten days. The very morning of our intended departure, I was looking into the court through a little round hole I had cleared for observation in the dust of one of the windows, believing I had observed signs of unusual preparation on the part of the household, when a carriage drove up, followed by two others, and Lord and Lady Hilton descended and entered, with an attendance of some eight or ten.

There was a great bustle in the house all day. Of course I felt uneasy, for if anything should interfere with our flight, the presence of so many would increase whatever difficulty might occur. I was also uneasy about the treatment my Alice might receive from the newcomers. Indeed, it might be put out of her power to meet me at all. It had been arranged between us that she should not come to the haunted chamber at the usual hour, but towards midnight.

I was there waiting for her. The hour arrived; the house seemed quiet; but she did not come. I began to grow very uneasy. I waited half an hour more, and then, unable to endure it longer, crept to her door. I tried to open it, but found it fast. At the same moment I heard a light sob inside. I put my lips to the keyhole, and called *"Alice."* She answered in a moment,

"They have locked me in."

The key was gone. There was no time to be lost. Who could tell what they might do to-morrow, if already they were taking precautions against her madness? I would try the key of a neighbouring door, and if that would not fit, I would burst the door open, and take the chance. As it was, the key fitted the lock, and the door opened. We locked it again on the outside, restored the key, and in another moment were in the haunted chamber. Alice was dressed, ready for flight. To me, it was very pathetic to see her in the shapes of years gone by. She looked faded and ancient, notwithstanding that this was the dress in which I had seen her so often of old. Her stream had been standing still, while mine had flowed on. She was a portrait of my own young Alice, a picture of her own former self.

One or two lights glancing about below detained us for a little while. We were standing near the window, feeling now very anxious to be clear of the house; Alice was holding me and leaning on me with the essence of trust; when, all at once, she dropped my arm, covered her face with her hands, and called out: "The horse with the clanking shoe!" At the same moment, the heavy door which communicated with this part of the house flew open with a crash, and footsteps came hurrying along the passage. A light gleamed into the room, and by it I saw that Lady Alice, who was standing close to me still, was gazing, with flashing eyes, at the door. She whispered hurriedly,

"I remember it all now, Duncan. My brain is all right. It is come again. But they shall not part us this time. You follow me for once."

As she spoke, I saw something glitter in her hand. She

had caught up an old Malay creese that lay in a corner, and was now making for the door, at which half a dozen domestics were by this time gathered. They, too, saw the glitter, and made way. I followed close, ready to fell the first who offered to lay hands on her. But she walked through them unmenaced, and, once clear, sped like a bird into the recesses of the old house. One fellow started to follow. I tripped him up. I was collared by another. The same instant he lay by his companion, and I followed Alice. She knew the route well enough, and I overtook her in the great hall. We heard pursuing feet rattling down the echoing stair. To enter my room and bolt the door behind us was a moment's work; and a few moments more took us into the alley of the kitchen garden. With speedy, noiseless steps, we made our way to the park, and across it to the door in the fence, where Wood was waiting for us, old Constancy pawing the ground with impatience for a good run.

He had had enough of it before twelve hours were over.

Was I not well recompensed for my long years of despair? The cold stars were sparkling overhead; a wind blew keen against us—the wind of our own flight; Constancy stepped out with a will; and I urged him on, for he bore my beloved and me into the future life. Close beside me she sat, wrapped warm from the cold, rejoicing in her deliverance, and now and then looking up with tear-bright eyes into my face. Once and again I felt her sob, but I knew it was a sob of joy, and not of grief. The spell was broken at last, and she was mine. I felt that not all the spectres of the universe could tear her from me, though now and then a slight shudder would creep through me, when the clank of Constancy's bit would echo sharply back from the trees we swept past.

We rested no more than was absolutely necessary; and in as short a space as ever horse could perform the journey, we reached the Scotch border, and before many more hours had gone over us, Alice was my wife.

CHAPTER 27

Freedom

HONEST Wood joined us in the course of a week or two, and has continued in my service ever since. Nor was it long before Mrs. Blakesley was likewise added to our household, for she had been instantly dismissed from the countess's service on the charge of complicity in Lady Alice's abduction.

We lived for some months in a cottage on the hillside, overlooking one of the loveliest of the Scotch lakes. Here I was once more tutor to my Alice. And a quick scholar she was, as ever. Nor, I trust, was I slow in my part. Her character became yet clearer to me, every day. I understood her better and better.

She could endure marvellously; but without love and its joy she could not *live,* in any real sense. In uncongenial society, her whole mental faculty had frozen; when love came, her mental world, like a garden in the spring sunshine, blossomed and budded. When she lost me, the Present vanished, or went by her like an ocean that has no milestones—she caring only for the Past, living only in the Past, and that reflection of it in the dim glass of her hope, which prefigured the Future.

We have never again heard the clanking shoe. Indeed, after we had passed a few months in the absorption of each other's society, we began to find that we doubted a great deal of what seemed to have happened to us. It was as if the gates of the unseen world were closing against us, because we had shut ourselves up in the world of the present. But we let it go gladly. We felt that love was the gate to an unseen world infinitely beyond that region of the psychological in which we had hitherto moved; for this love was teaching us to love all men, and live for all men. In fact, we are now, I am glad to say, very much like other people; and wonder, sometimes, how much of the story of our lives might be accounted for on the supposition that unusual coincidences had fallen in with psychological peculiarities. Dr. Ruthwell, who is sometimes our most welcome guest, has occasionally hinted at the sabre-cut as the key to all the mysteries of the story, seeing nothing of it was at least recorded before I came under his charge. But I have only to remind him of one or two circumstances, to elicit from his honesty an immediate confession of bewilderment, followed by silence; although he evidently still clings to the notion that in that sabre-cut lies the solution of much of the marvel. At all events, he considers me sane enough now, else he would hardly honour me with so much of his confidence as he does.

Having examined into Lady Alice's affairs, I claimed the fortune which she had inherited. Lord Hilton, my former pupil, at once acknowledged the justice of the claim, and was considerably astonished to find how much more might have been demanded of him, which had been spent over the allowance made from her income for her maintenance. But we had enough without claiming that.

My wife purchased for me the possession of my forefathers, and there we live in peace and hope. To her I owe the delight which I feel every day of my life in looking upon the haunts of my childhood as still mine. They help me to keep young. And so does my Alice's hair; for although much grey now mingles with mine, hers is as dark as ever. For her heart, I know that cannot grow old; and while the heart is young, man may laugh old Time in the face, and dare him to do his worst.

Afterword

READING a book by George MacDonald is (I think) like taking one's first trip to the Highlands of Scotland or reliving, in sudden spurts, the unforgettable moments of one's childhood. There is in his poems, adult faerie romances, parable-fairy-tales, novels, and devotional writings both the distant unknown and, at the same time, the familiar everyday world. One experiences, while reading MacDonald's fiction especially, the sensation of having gone far away as in a daydream and yet having remained at home, close to the warm coziness of the family circle and a roaring peat fire. And ultimately the reader is left with the conviction that here is a spinner of dreams and recorder of revelations who held strong beliefs about the meaning of life and how it should be lived.

I

The story of MacDonald's life and lengthy career (he wrote over fifty books from 1855 to 1897) begins in and constantly returns to his childhood. "I do not intend to carry my story one month beyond the hour when I saw my boyhood was gone and my youth arrived," writes MacDonald in the introduction to *Ranald Bannerman's Boyhood.* The boyhood attachments and experiences of the early years in his birthplace, Huntly, Aberdeenshire, in northern Scotland, seem to have been for him an irresistible source of wonder and magic. Throughout his later stories he recreates, with varying changes and additions, the events and people he knew at "The Farm"; in fact, there is not one of his books in which he does not somewhere refer to those early years.

For George MacDonald, childhood never ended. "I have had more pleasure when a grown man," he writes at age forty-eight in the introduction to his autobiographical novel *Wilfrid Cumbermede* (1872), "in a certain discovery concerning the ownership of an apple of which I had taken the ancestral bite when a boy, than I can remember to have resulted from any action of my own during my whole existence. . . . But I will rather shut out the fading west, the gathering mists, and the troubled consciousness of Nature altogether, light my fire and my pipe, and then try whether in my first chapter I cannot be a boy again in such a fashion that my ghostly companion, that is, my typical reader, will not be impatient to linger a little in the meadows of childhood ere we pass to the cornfields of riper years."

The phrase "meadows of childhood" significantly describes MacDonald's lifelong artistic and personal pursuit of the image of the child in his writings. Meticulously he attempts to reconstruct in the poetic language of his novels his recollections of his own moral development as a boy: his encounters with Nature and the closely knit life around him in Huntly. He sketches, for instance, in the opening chapter of *The Portent: A Story of Second Sight,** his filtered reminiscences of those early years of introspection, solitude, and active participation in dreams and visions. "From my very childhood," he recalls, "I had rejoiced in being alone. The sense of room about me had been one of my greatest delights." And then there follows a description of the Highland scene which, more than any other, haunted MacDonald's consciousness as a man and a writer: ". . . When my thoughts go back to those old years," he writes of Huntly, "it is not the house, not the family room, nor that in which I slept, that first of all rises before my inward vision, but that desolate hill, the top of which was only a wide expanse of moorland, rugged with height and hollow, and dangerous with deep, dark pools, but in many portions purple with large-belled heather, and crowded with cranberry and blaeberry plants. . . . There was one spot upon the hill, halfway between the valley and the moorland, which was my favorite haunt. . . . This was my refuge, my home within a home, my study—and, in the hot noons, often my sleeping chamber, and my house of dreams."

Such colorful passages of autobiographical reflection appear often in MacDonald's stories. As a novelist he frequently breaks into the story in order to share por-

*The title under which *Lady of the Mansion* was originally published. — ED

tions of his own life with the reader. In his second novel, *Alec Forbes of Howglen,* for example, he includes details of his boyhood at The Farm, "Howglen," and later describes in *Robert Falconer* and *Sir Gibbie* his days as a student at King's College, Aberdeen, in the 1840s. Filled with moving domestic scenes of kith and kin relationships and hints of his own spiritual awakening as a youth, MacDonald's thirteen Scottish novels (he wrote twelve set in England as well) reveal the warmth of human understanding and conservatory attitude toward all living things that is typical of everything he wrote: the belief that the deepest, mystical insights of life are not to be found in hidden obscurities but in ordinary, open, everyday contacts with the external world. The theme in all his fiction is the power of the commonplace. And even in his more symbolic tales, *Phantastes* and *Lilith,* it is his ability to transform ordinary places and events into visionary experiences that is MacDonald's special talent.

From childhood, MacDonald was attracted to the visionary aspects of life. Both of his parents possessed a Celtic tendency toward romance and song and a deep devotion to "clan-faith." His father was a staunch, determined man who was noted, if the stories told about him are true, for his humor, love of animals—particularly of horses, a love which his son shared—and storytelling gifts. Of his mother, Helen MacKay, who married George MacDonald, Senior, in 1822, not much is known. Reportedly she was a beautiful woman, sensitive and mystical by nature. She was descended from a distinguished line of military officers, politicians, and scholars; her elder brother, MacIntosh, was a friend of Sir Walter

Scott and her other brother, George MacKay, an officer who fought at Waterloo. He is said to have stimulated young George's love of the sea and his desire to travel. This first Mrs. MacDonald bore her husband six sons, four of whom survived. Seven years after her death, when George was eight, his father remarried and three sisters were added to the growing family.

George MacDonald was born on December 10, 1824. For a short time he lived in a stone house next to his grandmother's, not far from the town's busy square, where Huntly's local business and daily exchange took place: "Around the well," which stood in the center, records Greville MacDonald in his biography, "gathered the country women in grey cloak and white mutches, and the bare-headed maids, all with baskets on their arms with butter, eggs, cheese, and live fowls." It was a plain, agrarian world of "porridge and milk," one that "depended upon agriculture and handicrafts, and machinery," bleaching linen and spinning fine yarn: a crofter's existence in which MacDonald was reared, which he reflects in his novels.

The country scene he saw as a child had all the contrasting features one would find in any fairy-tale setting: a remote town ("The Little Grey Town") nestled in the circling glens of Strathbogie; the "rivers two" of the Bogie and Deveron, which flowed through the valley and around the citadel of Huntly Castle, overlooking the town below; and always the changing seasonal calls of Nature—the feminine moans of the wind whistling through the trees and glens, the long winter nights by peat fires, and the sudden spring breaking of the countryside into streaks of golden whins. It was—and still is—a "castle-building" atmosphere that invites dreams and visions.

When young George was two years old, his family and that of his Uncle James moved to Upper Pirriesmill to The Farm, or Bleachfield Cottage, as it was called then. There, in his upstairs gabled room with its secret stairway along the chimney and his skylight window open to the night sky, MacDonald began to build his own imaginary world: "I have a suspicion that my oldest memories are of dreams," he writes in *Ranald Bannerman's Boyhood:* "One I can recall, and it I will relate, or more properly describe, for there was hardly anything done in it. I dreamed it often. It was of the room I slept in, only it was narrower in the dream, and loftier, and the window was gone. But the ceiling was a ceiling indeed; for the sun, moon, and stars lived there. The sun was not a scientific sun at all, but one such as you see in penny picture-books." Graphically, Ranald describes the union of the planets: "I thought I awoke in the middle of the night, and lo! there was the room with the sun and the moon and the stars at their pranks and revels in the ceiling— Mr. Sun nodding and smiling across the intervening space to Mrs. Moon, and she nodding and smiling back to him with a knowing look, and the corners of her mouth drawn down. . . ."

But soon there came into the young boy's life also the harsh realities: the sudden death of his mother, the loss of two brothers, his own poor health, and the financial struggles which were to trouble him throughout most of his life. Out of these early years, however, there emerges the figure of his paternal grandmother, Isabella Robertson. Next to his father, to whom young George was deeply devoted, his grandmother seems to have had the strongest early influence on him. Known for her business sense, efficiency, benevolence (she adopted a family of four beggar children who had been abandoned), and pious dedication to the Missionar Kirk, she became the matriarchal head of the family and the model from which MacDonald later drew his concept of Wise Woman ("Mistress North Wind"), the ageless grandmother in his stories, who could reward and chastise at the same time. Although his grandmother is known to have destroyed some of the family records because she thought they were filled with "snares and wiles of Satan" (containing accounts of the family's Catholic past and clan treasures), she had a durable quality about her that George greatly admired. An amusing portrait of her appears as "Grannie" in the novel *Castle Warlock, A Homely Romance,* in which she tells her ghost story to young Cosmo and Aggie. The rural scene is typical of Aberdeenshire in winter:

One afternoon, clouds rising, and the wind blowing keen from the north, Cosmo left Glenwarlock for the village, to see how they were getting on. He tramped the two miles and a half in joyous conflict. The snow was deep and powdery, and struggle with windy space from incoherent feelings brought the blood to his cheeks and the sparkle to his eyes, and he entered the cottage radiant. He found Grannie sitting up in bed, and Aggie getting her tea. Setting on the table a bottle of milk he had brought—a luxury there in the winter—and some barley-meal scons Grizzie had made that morning, he dropped into Grannie's soft chair, and they had tea together. When tea was over, and Aggie was removing the things, her voice came feebly from the bed to Cosmo's ears, where he lay back luxurious in her great chair:

"Did ye dream only mair aboot the auld captain, Cosmo?" she asked.

At the age of sixteen George was sent to the Old Town Grammar School in Aberdeen, in preparation for entrance into King's College. He soon found himself thrust into a more sophisticated and competitive way of living. Winning a small bursary that gave him limited financial help, he took up "digs" at the top of the Spital Brae, in the College Bounds. As a student at Aberdeen, Mac-Donald was mentally alert but inclined at times to periods of moodiness and fits of depression, leading to constant self-searching, much like the hero of his novel *Robert Falconer* and the youth in his autobiographical poem "The Disciple," in which he traces some of his own spiritual conflicts and uncertainties. His outward appearance, however, was in striking contrast: he was observed wearing a "radiant tartan coat" and a controversial beard. As a student, MacDonald did well. He had a natural flare for science and philosophy, in both of which he took prizes, and probably only lack of funds prevented his entrance into the medical profession. On Sundays, he and other lads from the College attended Blackfriars Congregational Chapel, this at a time when the doctrines of Universalism and other "new views" had begun to challenge the established form of Scottish Calvinism. In the midst of adolescent turmoil, financial concerns, and the decision of a career, he tried to keep his boyhood vision of the dancing Planets alive; how to maintain his belief in universal goodness in the face of life's trials became the artistic and personal challenge that dominated the rest of his life.

II

The biographical background of MacDonald's *The Portent: A Story of the Inner Vision of the Highlanders, Commonly Called the Second Sight,* to give the book its full title, illustrates convincingly the extent to which the intermingling of autobiographical fact with fancy in MacDonald's fiction is characteristic of his storytelling genius. Throughout his literary career, MacDonald relied heavily on the personal experiences of his life for inspiration. In 1851, for example, he gave as a wedding gift to his wife the poem "Love me, Beloved," which appears later in his first publication, the dramatic poem *Within and Without* (1855). And shortly after the death of his brother and father, in 1858 he published his "adult faerie romance" *Phantastes,* which launched his career as a writer.

The year 1860 was a turning point for MacDonald and his family. With six children now to provide for (and a seventh on the way), MacDonald found himself besieged, as a father and a writer, with personal problems. His professorship at Bedford College in London gave him insufficient funds for his growing family, and the publishers had rejected his play *If I Had a Father.* Still trying to cope with the loss of his father, he was interrupted in his work by poor health. Encouraged, however, by the success of *Phantastes,* which had taken him only two months to write, MacDonald finished

"The Portent," drawing on memories of the years he had spent in Scotland before his marriage. And then, after weeks and months of struggle, records his son, there came a check for £300 from Lady Byron's executors, a legacy that the MacDonalds had not expected. About this time, the original version of "The Portent" was serialized in three parts ("Its Legend," "The Omen Coming On," "The Omen Fulfilled") in the *Cornhill Magazine* for May, June, and July 1860.

Although unlike "almost any other of his books," according to his son, the story "at once convinced friends and publishers" of MacDonald's "art in simple narrative." And four years later, in 1864 (after the successful publication of his first novel, *David Elginbrod,* in 1863), MacDonald published the expanded book version of the story. It was then that he added a happy ending, perhaps because he felt the pressure of his Victorian reading public, who would have liked a happy ending in the original. The serialized version left Duncan tormented by unrequited love for his lost Lady Alice:

> I know not whether she is alive or dead. I have sought her far and near; have wandered over England, France, and Germany, hopelessly searching; listening at tables-d'hote; lurking about madhouses; haunting theatres and churches; often begging my way from house to house in wild regions: I have not found her. I have made my way, unseen, to the ghostly chamber; have sat there through the phantom-crowded night: she was not amongst them. I have condensed my whole being into a single intensity of will, that she should come to me, and sustained it until I fainted with the effort: she did not come. I desisted, because I bethought

me what torture it must cause her, not to be able to obey it.

They say that Time and Space exist not, save in our thoughts. If so, then that which has been, is, and the past can never cease. She is mine, and I shall find her—what matters it where, or when, or how? Till then, my soul is but a moon-lighted chamber of ghosts; and I sit within, the dreariest of them all. When she enters, it will be a home of love; and I wait—I wait.

So ends the original version of the story.

From the date of its first publication, the strange exploration of the supernatural in *The Portent* caused readers to ask questions about the origin of the story and its relationship to MacDonald's own life. Unfortunately, however, what is known about its origin is mostly speculative. MacDonald himself, notes his son, "would reluctantly admit" that "he had himself no trace" of the gift of second sight. Reportedly, however, George MacDonald, Senior, did have such an experience of second sight when, records his grandson, he saw his son John walking near The Farm at Huntly on a "back road running up on to the moor" shortly after the boy's death. It is possible that MacDonald had this incident in mind when writing his romance.

Greville MacDonald also claims that the story partly incorporates events that may have taken place when, as a student, his father missed a session at King's College because of financial need. At that time he went to serve as a secretary and catalogued a neglected library "in a certain castle or mansion in the far North" (possibly Castle Sinclair in Thurso). Here, it has been further supposed, MacDonald fell in love with the daughter of the lord of the mansion, as Duncan does with Lady Alice, but was rejected because of class barriers.

To be sure, this romantic episode appears in other of MacDonald's novels—*Phantastes, David Elginbrod, Wilfrid Cumbermede, Donal Grant,* and *Lilith*—and yet similar frustrated romances were commonly to be found in novels of the period (in Charles Dickens's *Great Expectations,* for example) and MacDonald frequently repeated favorite scenes in his stories. Was this, however, the kind of romance which MacDonald had personally experienced or one that he feared he might experience someday, perhaps even after his marriage? When MacDonald's wife asked him "for the story's meaning," he replied: "You may make of it what you like. If you see anything in it, take it and I am glad you have it; but I wrote it for the tale." The important thing is that as a novelist MacDonald often made use of autobiographical material, but did so without obvious reference to himself. In this sense, his best biography is still—as he wished it—that to be found in his books.

Possibly MacDonald found in dreams and visions the ideal literary vehicle for transmitting the facts of his own life. When asked about his philosophical intentions as a writer, he would often quote, as he does in *The Portent,* his favorite aphorism from the German poet Novalis: "Our life is not a dream; but it may become a dream, and perhaps ought to become one." Paradoxically, MacDonald seems to be saying that the autobiographical aspects of a piece of fiction should not be seen in isolation, but that the story should be read as an aesthetic experience, as one would relate a dream to reality. This gives the reader full chance to sort out any parables of meaning in it by reflecting on the visionary content of the tale.

Such a subjective approach to reading fiction will not, of course, appeal to everyone; MacDonald himself anticipated that some adverse criticism might be leveled against him by those who admired the realism found in many of the more popular novels of the day. In defending the less admired "sensation novels" of the 1860s and the "romance" generally, he comments in his dedication of *The Portent* to his uncle: "I am well aware that such tales are not of much account, at present; and greatly would I regret that they should ever become the fashion. . . . But, seeing so much of our life must be spent in dreaming, may there not be a still nook, shadowy, but not miasmatic, in some lowly region of literature, where, in the pauses of labour, a man may sit down, and dream such a daydream as I now offer to your acceptance, and that of those who will judge the work, in part at least, by its purely literary claims?"

But what kind of truth or meaning, some may ask, is there in such "romances"? It is to be found, I think, as we see it developed in the theme of *The Portent: A Story of Second Sight:* the power of human love to overcome the baser passions of jealousy and hatred; and, if you like, the way in which two people in love can prove to be stronger than the dark omens of family superstition and the forces of psychic control: how love can defeat death.

In the final chapters of *The Portent,* there is much to suggest that MacDonald felt personally inspired to resolve the separation between Duncan and Lady Alice and to reunite them for more than literary or audience-appeal reasons. Here, again, the autobiographical implications are interesting. We see in the happy ending to the story MacDonald's deep commitment to marital bliss (the fairy-tale ending) and the fantasies of his own life, dating from his childhood. Curiously enough, in Margaret's death-trance, at the end, and Duncan's soul-searching séance with her, in which he asks for information about the whereabouts of his beloved, MacDonald returns to the wistful loves and haunts of his youth: the Highland paradisal scene for which he longed most:

> After removing the anxiety of my hostess, and partaking of their Highland breakfast, a ceremony not to be completed without a glass of peat whisky, I wandered to my ancient haunt on the hill. Thence I could look down on my old house, where it lay unchanged, though not one human form, which had made it home to me, moved about its precincts. I went no nearer. I no more felt that that was home, than one feels that the form in the coffin is the departed dead. I sat down in my old study-chamber among the rocks, and thought that if I could but find Alice, she would be my home—of the past as well as of the future—for in her mind my necromantic words would recall the departed, and we should love them together.

A reader coming to MacDonald's books for the first time may feel as if the ground in his stories has been covered before in some other world or period of time, feel as if one is meeting, after a long absence, an old friend or recognizing a familiar scene from one's childhood. It is, however, at such unexpected times that MacDonald's true genius as a maker of spiritual fantasies and a storyteller is most convincing. In spite of all the psychic explorations that go on in his novels—his books could be read as a guide to dream psychology—there is the quiet confidence that the unknown is being seen through the eyes of a child; there is nothing really to fear in the dark because the father is holding the child's hand. For finally, George MacDonald had no fear of death or dying, and it is for this reason, above all else, that his writings are of special value to the modern reader.

GLENN EDWARD SADLER

Point Loma College
San Diego, California